JEALOUSY

A RESTLESS SOULS WESTERN

MANUELA SCHNEIDER

Published by DS Productions

ISBN: 9798862773408

Created with Vellum

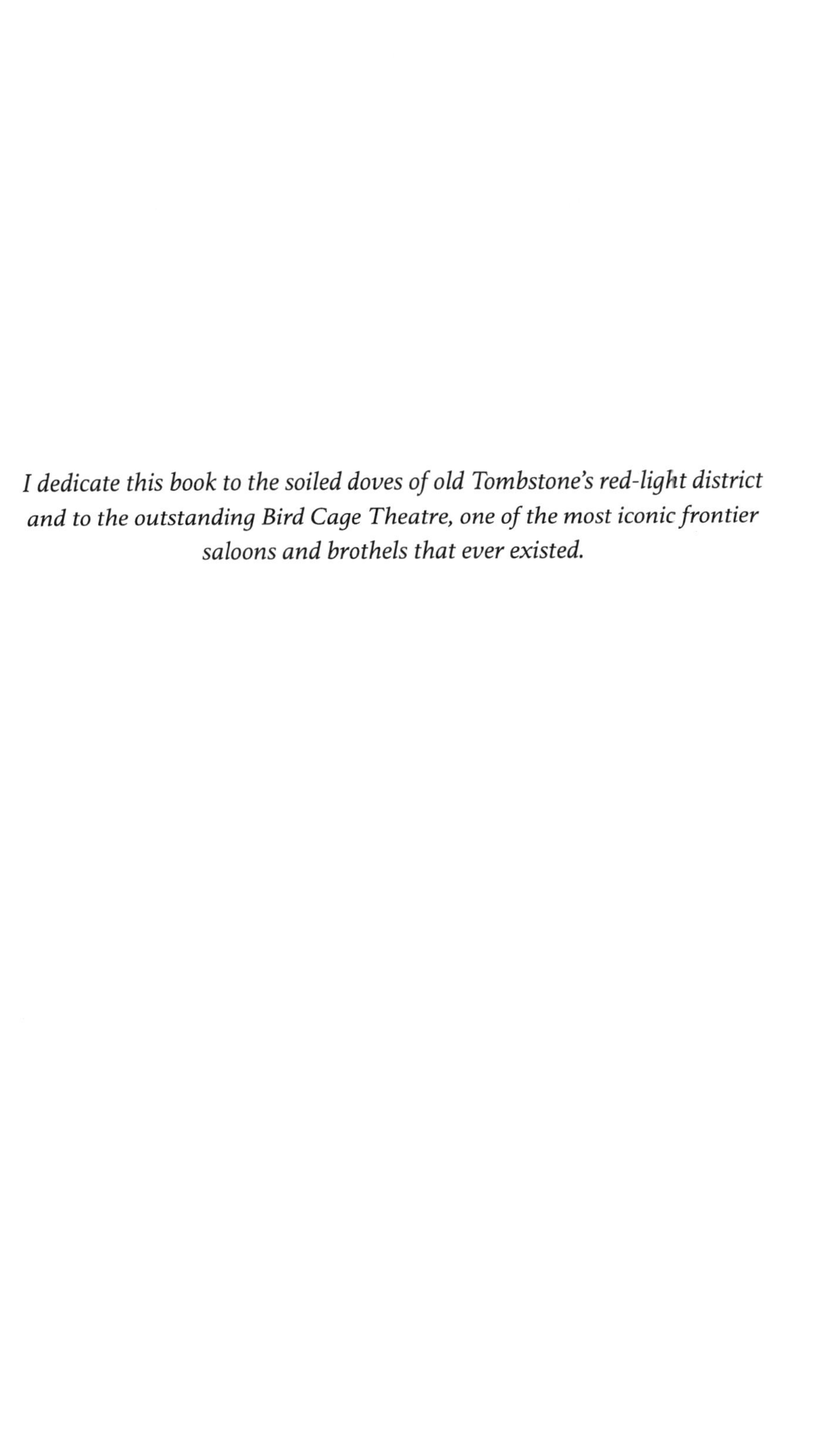

I dedicate this book to the soiled doves of old Tombstone's red-light district and to the outstanding Bird Cage Theatre, one of the most iconic frontier saloons and brothels that ever existed.

1

LATE NIGHT TRAGEDIES

The day's tourists were gone, and the two employees had locked up. Another day of strangers in shorts and flip-flops roaming the building ended. Except for the green light of the emergency exit signs, it was dark inside the Bird Cage Theatre. The many rooms of the wooden structure cracked occasionally as the structure cooled after the day's heat.

Since it was a weekday, not many visitors had explored the famous museum. Once the building had been the queen of entertainment in the bustling silver-mining camp called Tombstone. Nowadays, it is a well-known tourist attraction. But it is so much more than that. Very few of the people who walk through the different sections are aware that some of the guests and entertainers of yesteryear may never have left the Bird Cage Theatre.

Loud stomping footsteps interrupted the silence in the basement poker area. Footfalls rushed down the stairs, but nobody was visible. Silence descended again, then came a woman's giggle. If any of the daytime visitors had been around, they would have caught the whiff of rose perfume. Crashing filled the room as if furniture were being overturned. Then a high-pitched scream of terror pierced the lowest floor. Silence returned.

The poker table sat unoccupied with its stacks of coins, poker chips, and dollar bills on the faded green felt. A deck lay spread across the table, face up, waiting for the next hand. But something else appeared--a red stain spread on the table, moving toward the upturned deck, soiling the queen of hearts. The crimson liquid dripped over the table edge and collected in a puddle underneath. The sweet iron-like stench of blood filled the air. The table stood like a silent witness to one of the countless dramas which had taken place in Tombstone, Arizona.

When Rachel, one of the employees of the museum, opened up the following morning, she unlocked the doors and turned on all the lights. She made her usual morning rounds, inspecting all the rooms and displays to make certain nothing had been disturbed overnight. When she inspected the poker area, she saw nothing suspicious. The Bird Cage was ready for another day of welcoming visitors from all over the country.

2

THE FEAR OF A LITTLE GIRL

Despite her young age, eight-year-old Michelle Miller was a huge fan of Westerns. When her parents asked her what she wanted for her birthday, she wished for a very specific gift. Other kids might ask for a trip to Disney World or another amusement park, but little Michelle had something else in mind. She wanted to spend two days in Tombstone, Arizona. Knowing of her passion for Western movies, her parents agreed and planned a weekend getaway in that Old West town.

The family lived in Phoenix, not far from Tombstone. They drove the three hours to their destination, and checked into their hotel. When they arrived in town, the girl put on her pink cowboy boots and her mom bought her a stylish cowboy hat. Of course, a fake pistol in her girlish holster adorned with rhinestones had to complete the wannabe cowgirl's outfit.

First, the family enjoyed the comedy gun show on the main street of Tombstone. After the performer fired the first two shots, everyone else jumped at the loud noise, but Michelle didn't blink when the next shot rang out. The performer chose her to participate in the trick shooting using a water balloon. The audience clapped and cheered her performance, and her little face lit up with pure joy.

On the second day, her parents paid a visit to the Bird Cage Theatre. They'd told Michelle that the place would provide her a good education about some of the hardships the pioneers of those days had faced. Michelle felt rather subdued as soon as they entered the building. The blonde girl's eyes glanced around nervously.

"Are you okay, darling?" her mother asked, noticing apprehension in her daughter's blue eyes. "I'm sure you are a little tired after all your adventures yesterday, aren't you?"

Michael, Michelle's father, frowned. He wasn't used to his cheerful daughter being so quiet. "Well, maybe she's too young to appreciate artifacts in a museum," he told his wife. "Besides, it is kind of gloomy in here, and it looks like it was a mighty rowdy place in the old days. Look at all these bullet holes in the walls and ceiling, Dorothea."

They continued the tour of the museum, and walked behind the stage, but they didn't linger in that section very long. Neither of the parents wanted the girl to be upset by the coffins and the black funeral hearse displayed there.

"Oh my, that hearse reminds me of a fat, black, spider sitting in the corner waiting for its next victim," Dorothea Miller said, rubbing her upper arms, which Michelle could see had broken out in sudden goosebumps.

Even her husband looked uncomfortable around the display of death and undertaker's equipment. "Wonder why they even show these kinds of artifacts in a former theater," he mumbled.

The family continued their stroll through the Bird Cage, slowly walking down the stairs toward the basement where the most famous poker game in the Wild West had been held. At least, that was what the modern-day owners claimed in the brochure.

Michelle followed them hesitantly. It seemed as if something was keeping her from setting one foot in front of the other, holding her back from entering the lowest floor. Her mother gestured to her husband not to read out the signs in front of the two prostitution chambers opposite the stairs. It wasn't necessary for an eight-year-old girl to study information about the world's oldest trade. Mr. Miller nodded silently to indicate he understood.

When Michelle set foot on the last step and turned toward the poker area, she stopped dead still. Her eyes grew huge, and she stared unblinking at the gambling area.

"Darling, do you want to throw a coin onto the poker table? Maybe some cowboy will come and play poker with it," her mother suggested with a warm smile.

But the girl didn't react. Instead, she turned pale as a ghost and her hands trembled.

Her mother frowned. "What's the matter, Michelle? Anything wrong?"

The girl pointed to the table. "Mommy, there's so much blood. It smells bad. Somebody got killed."

Her mother looked at the poker area, but all she saw were faded cards, poker chips, coins, and crumpled dollar bills. "What blood, honey?"

The girl's eyes filled with tears. Her shoulders heaved. "The entire table is full of it. Why don't you see it? I want to leave. Please let's go. This place is full of bad people watching me," she stuttered and sobbed hard.

Her father stepped behind the girl and hugged her. "What's wrong with you, little princess? Why are you so scared?" When he touched her, he was shocked at how cold her skin was. Goosebumps covered her bare arms. He felt her shivering like a leaf.

Mr. Miller turned to his wife. "Let's leave right now, Dorothea. Something is scaring the wits out of her. I don't see anything, but we both know that Michelle sometimes sees things that others don't."

Dorothea Miller nodded, returning her husband's serious look.

All three turned and walked quickly through the adjoining rooms and the gift shop. Only when they stepped into the warm afternoon sun did the girl relax. "I tell you what Michael, I'll talk to the child psychologist first thing Monday morning and arrange an appointment for her. These weird reactions have been going on for way too long."

With a worried expression, Mr. Miller nodded in agreement. The girl seemed relieved to have escaped the building but couldn't regain her cheerful mood. She turned frequently as if she feared someone followed her. Her parents left town three hours earlier than they had originally planned.

It was early afternoon when they headed back home to Phoenix. Little Michelle turned backward in the seat and stared at the Bird Cage Theatre as her father left the parking lot. The girl saw her reflection in the rear windshield--a mask of fear.

3

ARRIVING IN THE USA

After a long flight, Billy checked into the Hilton Airport Hotel in Phoenix, Arizona. He thought the flight from Munich with a long layover in Atlanta would never end. He recalled how he loved traveling when he was in his early twenties but now that he'd reached his mid-forties, too many people around him aggravated him. These days, the rage that built inside him as he stood in line for the airport check-in counters was no stranger to him.

He often wondered if people had always behaved so thoughtlessly, or if a new level of selfishness had developed in mankind that he hadn't been aware of before. This vacation was supposed to be fulfilling a long-time dream, so he had no choice but to endure the torture of countless hours in the air for the sake of reaching the Wild, Wild West. Since his boyhood days, Billy wanted to explore the southwest part of the United States, with its mysterious ghost towns and western history. He intended to cruise down the scenic highways on a rented Harley-Davidson.

After quitting his successful management position at a well-known car dealership, he planned a three-month vacation. For the first time in his life, he would be following his own dreams. If he didn't do it now, he likely never would. Billy had arrived at a turning point in his life and was ready to start over again.

"Here's your room key, sir. Your room is on the third floor. Breakfast will be served from six thirty to ten o'clock. In case you need anything else, you may dial zero on your room phone. Oh, before I forget, our restaurant offers room service as well. Dial twelve for Joe's Barbeque. Thanks for choosing the Hilton for your stay."

The front desk employee handed him the key card and pointed toward the elevator. Billy carried his backpack and crossed the tastefully decorated lobby. He stepped into the elevator, glanced at his key card, and pushed the third button from the bottom. Knowing that he would be traveling by motorcycle he had decided against bringing a suitcase. There wouldn't be enough space for his designer wardrobe in the saddlebags of the Harley. Generally, Billy was dressed quite stylishly, but this time he wasn't trying to impress anyone. This vacation would be a taste of freedom and the start of a new and simpler life.

Billy unlocked the door to his room, 308, and switched on the lights. The interior was decorated in brown and beige and the king size bed, covered in fluffy pillows, looked mighty tempting. He quickly unpacked all the necessities which were needed for a one-night stay.

Hearing his stomach growl, he decided to give room service in this hotel a try. He picked up the phone, dialed the restaurant downstairs, and ordered a buffalo burger with sweet potato fries and coleslaw. This would be the first western meal of his trip, and the thought of it made his mouth water.

He grabbed his toiletry bag and walked into the bathroom. After a relaxing hot shower under the massaging jets, he felt much better. He quickly dressed in shorts and a fresh T-shirt and combed his wet hair. The thick curls fell back over his forehead in their usual rebellious ways.

Billy grinned at the reflection in the mirror. "Now what would Mr. Schmidt say if he could see you with this far-from-perfect hairstyle, unshaven, and ragged-looking?" he asked himself with a chuckle.

The mirror reflected a smile growing on Billy's face, as he felt deep satisfaction at the state of his life.

God knew the past seven months had been harsh enough. At work, upper management constantly exerted increasing pressure to sell more and more cars. He caught his beloved wife with his boss-man, and the nasty divorce after that had almost broken him. That jerk sure as hell had a weird way of thanking him for the twelve years of excellent service he had given to the company. Taking away another man's wife was absolutely unacceptable for Billy--but after thinking through all of it, he was better off without her, anyway.

This vacation--which he nicknamed the Ride of Freedom--was to be a reward just for him. "I haven't attended to my own needs for so many years, being the least rewarding to myself. It's about time for it, Billy-boy."

A knock at the door interrupted his gloomy self-reflection. He opened it, and the smell of southwestern cuisine wafted into the room. The waiter rolled the room service cart through the door and presented his meal. He arranged the tray on the table beside the TV, raising each cloche and saying the name of the dish Billy had ordered.

Billy signed the tab and gave the fellow a generous tip. The waiter opened the door. "Hang the Do Not Disturb sign on to the door-knob, will you please?"

The waiter did so and shut the door. Billy turned on the TV, picked up the tray, and sat on the bed. He munched on the delicious food. It felt good to unwind from the strain of traveling for twenty hours.

Little did he know this first night in Arizona would lead him into the wildest adventure of his life and into dangers he could never before have imagined.

4

COCHISE COUNTY

After a big cowboy breakfast, Billy picked up his rental Harley the following morning. Although he had neglected his hobby for many years, he was a well-experienced rider. It didn't take long before he was on the road cruising through the landscape full of impressive saguaro cactuses surrounding Tucson. He enjoyed the rumble of the engine and the warm wind on his face. For the first time in many months, Billy had the feeling of being able to breathe freely.

His first stop took him to the old Tucson film studios, where they had shot countless movies which he recalled from his youth. He joined one of the tours explaining the different locations among the buildings where epic movie scenes had been filmed then watched the professional stunt show. The stuntman performed the classic tricks, like being shot down from a church tower, taking a high fall, or running from the burning shed. The big surprise about the shed was how it ignited in flames seconds after the stunt men came running out of it. The visitors cheered, and Billy was mightily impressed right along with them.

When he walked over to the restaurant to grab some lunch, he met one of the performers. "That was an amazing show," he told the man, still dressed in his western garb. "I'm truly impressed, although some of your stunts look rather dangerous."

The fellow, perhaps in his late forties, smiled back at him. "Glad you enjoyed it. Where are you from? Your accent sounds European."

Billy laughed. "You got that right. I'm German. Arrived here yesterday evening after an endless flight. I rented a Harley and plan to explore Arizona and meet up with some people whom I know only from Facebook."

"I see," the stuntman said. "My name is Eddie McKechnie. I reckon you'll visit the main tourist spots like the Grand Canyon, Sedona, or parts of our famous Route 66, right?"

Billy shook his head. "To be honest I visited all those spots many years ago during my honeymoon. Now that I'm freshly divorced, I feel no urge to revisit those places so soon."

Eddie laughed. "Quite understandable."

Billy went on, "You know, I read a lot of books and did some research about the Gold Rush and the silver mining history of Arizona and California. I intend to travel the less crowded routes. I'd rather see some interesting ghost towns or pioneer cemeteries than face hundreds of people stepping on my toes at the rim of the Grand Canyon. I need some alone--time to come to terms with this new chapter in my life. I don't feel like facing old memories."

Eddie nodded his head once. "I tell you what, if you want to get some impressions about the pioneer days, take that motorcycle and ride along the ghost town trail in Cochise County. You will come across settlements from the silver rush days. Each grave marker in those cemeteries tells its own story. Then there is Fort Bowie where Geronimo was held prisoner before being deported all the way to Florida. You'll find a lot of amazing history of the Apache as well as the pioneers." The man took a sip of his iced tea. "And then there is, of course, the world-famous Tombstone. One shouldn't miss out on that town when traveling to Arizona. It is a must-see."

"I intend to spend a few days in Tombstone and explore the area from there."

"That's a good idea. In case you haven't booked your room yet check out the San Jose House. It's the oldest boarding house in town and belonged to Ed Schieffelin. He was the prospector who founded Tombstone. My wife and I own it and we remodeled it to modern standards but tried to keep the Old West rugged look."

"Actually, since I haven't booked a hotel room yet I might as well give it a try. I prefer accommodations which give me the authentic feel of the historical place."

"Great, I'll let my wife know and make sure she holds the nicest room for you. As for feeling like you've been transported back in time, you'll surely experience that in our town. To a certain degree, it might even feel eerie."

Billy searched the man's face, not knowing how to respond to that. But his new acquaintance avoided his gaze and waved at the waitress for his check. He scribbled down the address of the San Jose House and the phone number of his wife Anne. "I'll reserve the room for you by text. Just give her a holler when you're about to arrive in town. I can imagine that you'd like to visit a couple of spots on the way to Tombstone."

Billy thanked the man, paid for his food, and continued his slow stroll through the old Tucson studios. He took a lot of pictures on the set of *The High Chaparral*. It had been his favorite show for a long time. Billy had been thrilled when a German TV channel enhanced the quality of the episodes and broadcast them again in the late eighties, along with other Western shows like *Dr. Quinn, Medicine Woman* and *Bonanza* that they showed in the nineties.

It was late afternoon when he hit the road again toward Cochise County. Cruising slowly as he took in the scenery of the Sonoran Desert around him, his trip required a little over one and a half hours to get to the touristy settlement of Tombstone. He rode along Fremont Street past Boot Hill Cemetery. Less than five minutes after reaching the Tombstone city limits, he found the San Jose Boarding House. He got off the motorcycle and checked his mobile phone for the provided key code, which he needed to release the room key from the small lockbox next to the first door of the building.

He opened the door to his guest room, which turned out to be a tidy apartment including a kitchenette with an attached dining room, a nice air-conditioned bedroom, and a seating area with a flatscreen TV. The kitchenette offered a small fridge, a microwave, and--to his delight--a modern coffee maker. The compact bathroom had the rustic, yet charming look of the Old West. Billy read a small, framed letter which hung on the wall next to the sink.

DEAR GUEST,

Welcome to our epic town of Tombstone.

We are happy to have you here in the oldest boarding house in town. The San Jose House was established in 1881 during Tombstone's heyday. Although we remodeled our accommodations with the greatest of care, the age of the building can't be denied. The stains you might see in your bathtub and sink aren't evidence of a lack of cleaning but result from years of buildup of the many different minerals in the soil and water in this town. Please remember that the history of this mining community is based on those mineral deposits.

If you need anything, please feel free to contact your host, Anne McKechnie. There's a list with suggestions for dining and things to do in Tombstone on your living room table. We hope you have a pleasant stay in the Town Too Tough to Die.

Your San Jose House management

BILLY SMILED. He didn't mind the well-used look of the tub and sink. He liked the rugged appearance of the building and the southwestern interior design. The furniture looked comfortable, and he immediately felt at home. Billy had always preferred the coziness of smaller places to stay, unlike his ex-wife, who was more the five-star hotel type of woman. If it was up to her, it had to be the Hyatt Regency, at least.

After unpacking his belongings, he changed into a fresh T-Shirt and walked into the famous Allen Street only two blocks away. It was a normal weekday, and the town didn't seem too busy. Most shops were already closed, but Billy didn't mind because he would have more than enough time to explore the town during his stay. He walked straight into the Crystal Palace Saloon, where he intended to eat a nice dinner to celebrate his arrival in Tombstone.

Before he took a seat, he strolled around the walls of the saloon and marveled at the original roulette table which was displayed against the wall. The beige and maroon old-style wallpaper with its ornamental design and paintings of shady ladies added to the saloon's atmosphere. The bar itself was an impressive piece of carpentry craftsmanship built from carved hardwood. Billy was quite astonished at the wide array of bottles displayed behind the bar, offering every possible alcoholic beverage, even German Jägermeister.

The waitresses working behind the bar were not hard to look at. They were quite young and wore daring saloon outfits with red corsages and net stockings that emphasized their curves. "Welcome to the Wild West," Billy mumbled.

"Howdy, Cowboy, my name is Lisa, and I'm your waitress for today. Can I get you something to drink?"

"I'll take a cold draft beer, and I also need the menu."

"All righty. Oh, before I forget, we are out of buffalo burgers, but there is still some of Today's Special, which is prime rib with baked potato, baked beans, and a house side salad."

"You know what, that sounds excellent. I'll take Today's Special, medium rare, please. And if possible, with a biscuit and some butter to go along."

"Okay, I'll be right back with your cold beer."

Billy leaned back and glanced over at the huge TV screen. He couldn't hear the sound but recognized the scenes right away. *How epic. Here you are, seated in a saloon in Tombstone watching the movie* Tombstone. *You should have done this years ago.*

Billy felt a bit bitter about having always put himself at the end of the queue for the sake of others who had never shown gratitude for it. One thing was sure, he was determined to change that from now on.

5

MEETING NEW FRIENDS

The following morning Billy strolled up and down Allen Street, exploring the stores. He wasn't a shopping kind of guy, but, to his surprise, he ended up buying a few things. A new western belt with silver conchos and horsehair braided work caught his eye. He also bought a new Stetson hat with a silver band and a pair of new Wranglers for sale at the most reasonable price he'd ever seen. It felt good to spend some money on himself for a change.

Billy went back to the boarding house, changed into his new denims, and picked up his cowboy hat from the table. He stepped outside, locked the door, and decided to watch one of the gun shows in town. He bought a ticket for Wyatt Earp's Oriental Saloon and Theater. The building hosted a gun show which re-enacted events from inside that very building or just in front of it during the wild days of this place. While he waited for the entertainment to start, he admired the old hardwood floor and the tin ceiling, wondering if they were original. A long, impressive, antique bar ran the length of the right wall.

The re-enactors were quite talented, and they wanted to portray the historical events accurately. The crew acted out three different episodes which took place during the months that Wyatt Earp ran the Oriental Saloon in late 1881. For the audience, it was instructive to see that someone always got shot in those historical scripts. However, Billy knew that there was cruel truth behind those stories.

After the show, Billy stepped up to the fellow who played Wyatt Earp. "May I ask you, did these events really take place according to the script of the show?"

The guy was a few inches taller than Billy, but he seemed friendly. "Dang sure, sir. This town has kept a lot of its historical papers in the city hall and museums. Historians have researched most of the gunfights in addition to the famous one at the O.K. Corral. Tombstone was a mighty rowdy place in the old days. Hollywood wants to make us believe that the typical gunfight took place in the streets at high noon. That ain't true. Most fights occurred right in the saloons or brothels. The law of the gun ruled the pioneer days. It was a matter of survival to be as fast as possible with a six-shooter in hand. I doubt that two opponents willing to kill each other would have taken time to walk out into the street, march forty feet apart and wait for some onlookers to arrive before shooting at each other. That's the Hollywood version and has likely not much to do with the reality of the old days."

Billy laughed. "That makes perfect sense to me. By the way, I really enjoyed your performance."

"Is this your first visit to Tombstone?" the actor asked.

"Yes. I flew in from Germany, and so far, I'm enjoying this vacation very much. I have some Facebook friends from around here, and I hope to meet some of them in person. By the way, talking of making friends, where do you keep your tip jar?"

Wyatt, as his fellow actors called him, reached behind a makeshift bar near the entrance and held up a brass jar. "Now remember, this is for tipping and not for spitting," he added with a hearty laugh. "Hey if you feel like coming back this evening, I'll be dealing at the faro table and teaching folks the games of the West. We'll probably start after the last show around five o'clock."

"Sounds interesting. I'll be staying at least a week so I wouldn't mind giving it a try to learn some Old West gambling. See you later, then."

Billy tipped his new Stetson and left the Oriental Saloon. He looked across the street and noticed a separate building. It was a typical southwestern adobe structure, and the big sign in front of it read "Bird Cage Theatre."

Billy had heard about the place and intended to visit it later this week. The Courthouse Museum held the top position on his bucket list, so he took a left turn and strolled along the boardwalk in the direction of Toughnut Street. He had to stop as the red painted stagecoach rattled along the paved side street. Somehow the sound of it gave Billy a homey feeling. He made a mental note to ride in one of the coaches while he was in town.

6

THE COURTHOUSE MUSEUM

Billy was quite impressed as he walked toward the old Victorian building. It was likely the biggest in the entire town besides Schieffelin Hall close to the San Jose House. The brick-red stone stood out in charming contrast to the wide windowsills. A small tower added to its impressive looks. When he read travel magazines about this pioneer town, the Courthouse Museum was always mentioned as the one with the finest collection of artifacts from Tombstone's early days.

Billy paid the admission fee and stepped into the first room. Glass cabinets held artifacts of Doctor Goodfellow, Wyatt Earp, and the notorious Doc Holliday. Billy strolled from room to room. When he entered the courtroom, a sudden dizziness made him grab the balustrade in front of the judge's bench. A whisper rustled through the room.

"What in the world," he mumbled. *Must be the warm weather and unusually high elevation.*

He looked around, feeling rather uncomfortable. For some reason, the court room seemed familiar to him. It looked like the ones in Western movies, but bigger. Next to it was a hallway which led into a chamber with a writing desk full of law books. As soon as he left the courtroom, the dizziness vanished. Billy shook his head. He walked toward the posh salon where a huge table was covered in fine porcelain dishes, silver plates, cutlery, and lead crystal glassware. One could imagine a formal dinner would be held here at any time.

"This looks quite sophisticated for a pioneer town," he mumbled. The quality of the furniture and household items surprised Billy. He would have expected it in a nobleman's home in historic London but not here in a rustic pioneer town. "Wonder if the judge once lived on this upper floor. It sure looks like a prominent household."

When he walked downstairs again, he gazed back at the beautifully built old stairway. The steps were worn, but the railing carved from oak still carried the elegance of its former splendor.

The museum section in the back held a lot of mining equipment, as well as an impressive collection of the chemicals used for silver processing and making medication. Billy always thought that mining was like chiseling the silver out of rocks. Apparently, and to his surprise, a lot more work was needed to process it. The ore had to be stamped with large presses then processed with a variety of chemicals to extract the silver. Labor must have been hard in those days. Billy could barely imagine lifting the heavy chisels and hammers or working with them on twelve-hour shifts.

"They thought this to be the promise of a better tomorrow, and you complained about selling cars eight hours a day wearing a fine suit and being entitled to a full six weeks of paid vacation," he mumbled, suddenly embarrassed about his ungratefulness.

A door on the left led visitors into the Courthouse Museum's open courtyard. Billy stepped into the glaring afternoon sun, and, to his surprise, he saw a gallows with three ropes dangling. *Probably only for effect,* he thought.

As he was about to turn around to walk inside the building again, he caught a black shadow on one of the ropes. "What the...." But as he stared back at the spot, the shadow was gone. "Must have been an optical illusion of the sun casting shadows behind the building," he mumbled.

Billy left the Courthouse Museum, but the place left him

thoughtful. He pulled his mobile phone from his hip pocket and called his Facebook friend Magnus Alberts. He picked up after a couple of rings.

"Hey Magnus, this is Billy Grienmuller from Germany. I arrived in Tombstone last evening, and I was wondering if you would like to join me for a snack and a cold one. It would be great to finally meet you in person, my friend."

Magnus agreed immediately, and they decided to meet at Big Nose Kate's Saloon.

Less than half an hour later, Magnus walked through the door, and Billy waved him over to his corner table. The two men greeted each other with a hearty slap on the shoulder and sat down to order their food.

7

SOME OF THE DARK HISTORY

Billy studied his friend's appearance. He was an impressive character with long, blond hair and steely blue-gray eyes. Magnus was tall, slim, and reflected his Scandinavian roots. Billy had been following the man's blog for almost two years. He had traveled most of the US by motorcycle with his four-legged sidecar partner, Chaco, a black stray dog he rescued from the lonely wilderness from the Chaco Canyon area.

"So, how do you like the Town Too Tough to Die?" Magnus wanted to know.

"It sure is something else. Seems very authentic. I watched one of the gunfight shows today and paid a visit to the Courthouse Museum."

Magnus nodded thoughtfully. "Well, as far as authenticity goes, a lot of the original buildings burned down in two big fires over the years. A lot of the structures have been rebuilt since then. Of course, they are still old but some of them aren't from the founding days and were rebuilt after Wyatt Earp and Doc Holliday left town. As for the Courthouse Museum, that place has an amazing collection, and those artifacts are definitely more original than some of the movie props displayed in many of the places around here."

Billy studied his friend's serious face. "You don't like the touristy stuff here in town, do you?"

"Naw, not really. See, I'm very much into history. Tombstone wouldn't exist if not for the miners and if not for a prospector called Ed Schieffelin. He was of German heritage, by the way. All those crooks and law dogs came to town because it was already a thriving mining camp. It kind of annoys me that people pay more attention to the Tombstone portrayed in Hollywood movies instead of learning the true history of this place. Now, don't get me wrong, I do think that the movie is one of the best Westerns ever produced, if not the best. Acting, dialogues, shooting scenes, everything was brilliantly done. It just upsets me that people think that this movie reflects the truth. It's close, but it leaves out a lot of true history, and it sure doesn't offer any praise to the miners who deserve it."

Billy took a sip of his cold beer. "I think I understand what you mean. We have a lot of mining history in central Germany. It's surely one of the toughest jobs in this world. A lot of Germany's success as an industrial nation is based on stone and brown coal mining. But the government wasn't grateful to our miners because they closed down most of the mines, leaving thousands of people jobless. Some of those men were in the fourth or fifth generation to work in those mines. Now they have to learn new professions, and some of the elderly fellows are stranded in jobs they can't identify with. It's hard to learn new tricks when you're past fifty. One thing I know--miners are a special group of people."

"You got that right, my friend. If you want to learn the true history of Tombstone, I can take you down to one of the biggest mines here. Give you a tour and explain to you about the true hardship which they faced. Some of those mines have up to six levels of tunnels--the entire town is undermined with shafts that run mile after mile into the surrounding hills. Some of them are dug more than four hundred feet below ground, if not more. This entire landscape is like a Swiss cheese."

Billy's tone expressed surprise. "Wow, I had no idea the mines were so extensive or ran so deep."

Magnus continued, "You selected a good starting place by visiting the Courthouse Museum, since a lot of their artifacts give you an idea about silver processing. Believe me, it is very different if you're more than four hundred feet underground, and you see chambers the size of cathedrals chiseled out by hand."

"Man, I would love to see that. Count me in on your tour. One of my ancestors was a miner, and I think I owe it to him to learn more about it."

"What else do you wanna see during your stay here?"

"I definitely want to tour the Ghost Town Trail and visit Fort Bowie. I read books about Geronimo, and I'm sure it feels special to walk the grounds where he was captured. Oh, and, of course, I want to visit the Bird Cage Theatre. I read a lot about it, and it seems to be another must-see in Tombstone."

"Sure is," said Magnus. "It's one of the few buildings that never burned down. Most likely it didn't catch fire thanks to the adobe walls. So, when you enter the Bird Cage, you set foot into the true history of this town, just like in them mines. Most items displayed there are authentic, well, except for the movie casket next to the Black Moriah. I think they bought it off the film crew after they were done shooting that movie. Didn't even shoot it in town but way out at Mescal movie set."

"What in the world is the Black Moriah?" Billy wanted to know.

The waitress stepped up to their table to serve their food. If Billy expected Magnus to eat a typical cowboy dinner, he was mistaken. Like the sophisticated traveler he was, Magnus had ordered a Caesar salad. After the server left their table, he took a few bites, then went on explaining about the Black Moriah.

"It's the name of the funeral hearse displayed behind the stage in the Bird Cage. It was the last ride for most people in this town during its heyday. Even the victims of the O.K. Corral gunfight were transported out to Boot Hill in that very hearse. The undertaker owned it and it is decorated with sterling silver and sheet gold. The Black Moriah is one out of five identical models from that era, but it is said that the one inside the Bird Cage is the only one that still exists. The

Hunley family who owns the museum claims that the insurance judged its worth at two million dollars. Quite possible, considering the fact that some of the most famous characters in pioneer history had their last ride in that vehicle."

Billy swallowed a bite. "Now that Bird Cage place, what exactly was it? Some folks say it was a theater, others claim it was a saloon and gambling parlor."

Magnus nodded. "It was all of that and more. It was meant to be a theater of fine entertainment for the town families. However, that didn't work for the owners, as no decent woman would set foot in that building. Hutchinson and his wife, the owners, feared for their income when they realized that married couples would likely not be willing to spend their money there. They both used to work in a Cabaret on the east coast and hoped to strike it rich with the new entertainment house in town. Unfortunately, there was too much drinking and rowdy behavior going on during the shows. Hutchinson feared losing all his money. It didn't take long before the shady ladies declared the building their favorite stomping ground. Hutchinson was no fool. He quickly understood he would probably draw a bigger crowd of male visitors if he allowed those kinds of women inside the Bird Cage. He had no doubt that the miners and other workers of Tombstone would be willing to spend their hard-earned money and silver on women and the outstanding variety of liquor he served. The next thing he added was a gambling section and prostitution cribs."

Billy almost choked on his bite of meatloaf. "Wait a minute are you saying that the Bird Cage was a brothel?"

"Yes, Billy. It was a brothel and a gambling place, a saloon, and the town's theater. I think they spelled the name in the European rather than the American fashion to make it seem fancier. It hosted the poker game with the highest stakes ever, not only in town but in the entire Southwest, they say. The who's who of 1880s showbiz, if you wanna call it that, made it a point to schedule their tours for an appearance on that very stage. Local legend holds that the world-famous opera singer Enrico Caruso did a stint at the Bird Cage Theatre."

"Oh wow, I can hardly wait to set foot into it. This sounds very intriguing. How come they named the place Bird Cage Theatre? This is rather odd."

"The girls serving the guests in the old days wore daring costumes which they often adorned with different-colored feathers. Above the main theater room and the stage area, the owner had boxes constructed which could hold from two to four people. Of course, those provided a very special view of the stage, but even more so, they were used as small prostitution cribs with a tiny cot, a lamp for dim light, and velvet curtains which could be closed for more privacy. The girls with their feathers must have reminded the guests of birds in a cage up there in those boxes. Legend goes that this is where the theater got its name. It also inspired a composer to write the famous song about 'A Bird in a Gilded Cage.' "

"Magnus, you are the best tour guide I could have found. It is unbelievable how much you know about the history of this town, considering the fact that you've only lived here for a few years."

Billy's new friend looked rather serious as he put his fork down. "I've got to warn you, Billy. As fascinating as Tombstone is, it can be dangerous around here. This town has two sides. Many people come here for a visit and don't pay attention to the dark side of town."

"The dark side? Is there a dangerous area I should avoid?"

"Oh no, I'm not talking about the danger in certain streets. Of course, we have our share of alcoholics and druggies, but that's not what I mean. It's difficult to explain, but Tombstone's past is somehow still alive, and I'm not talking about the re-enactments. Some folks who come here get drawn into it. Some people get mesmerized by this town and find it hard to leave. Of course, it's a neat little town--especially if you are into western history, but there's much more to it. A lot of people have the eerie feeling that they are coming home after a long absence. Strange things happen around here, Billy, especially in the old buildings."

"I don't get what you're referring to, but I admit I had a weird feeling when I visited the courtroom of the Courthouse Museum. Almost felt as if I knew the place, as if I'd stood trial there. Of course, that's nonsense because this is my first visit to Cochise County."

Magnus pushed away his empty salad bowl and took a sip of his beer. When he spoke again his face was deadly serious. "You might think I'm crazy, but this place is haunted. Do you know why they call it the Town Too Tough to Die?"

"Yes, because it's still alive and still thriving despite the end of the silver rush. People haven't given up on Tombstone, have they?"

"Very true. I'm afraid the locals aren't the only ones who haven't given up on Tombstone. This town had a reputation of having a man for breakfast. This was an extremely violent place and both good and bad men got killed every single day. Fights erupted over a deck of cards or the favors of one of the soiled doves. It didn't take much to get killed in those streets. Many others committed suicide, especially the prostitutes. Countless folks died of disease. Boot Hill is not the only cemetery. It ran out of room the first three or four years of the town's existence. They call the other one the 'new cemetery,' but it's almost as old as Boot Hill. So, if you visit the Bird Cage Theatre tomorrow, be aware that during its eight and a half years of existence, twenty-six people got killed in that very building."

"What? You gotta be kidding me. I thought it was a theater and not a slaughterhouse."

Magnus shook his head. "I'm serious, Hoss. You may or may not believe in paranormal events, but the fact is that every single TV show involved in the spooky genre knows this place for good reason. *Ghost Hunters*, *Paranormal Files*, and others have shot footage in that building--and not only once. They keep coming back for more. Guess why."

"Well, now I'm even more eager to see the place. Can hardly wait."

Magnus checked his watch. "Well, I better head back to the house. Time to walk Chaco around the block."

The two men decided to meet for a motorcycle ride out along the Ghost Town Trail two days later. Billy looked forward to it since Magnus seemed to be a walking encyclopedia of the history of Cochise County, and Billy loved to learn about the places he visited.

Besides that, Magnus proved to be a real decent fellow to "ride the river with."

The things he heard about the Bird Cage Theatre gave Billy food for thought. Walking back to the San Jose House didn't take him past the theater, now one of the most famous pioneer-era museums. However, for some reason he was more aware of the building at the east end of Allen Street than he had been earlier in the afternoon.

This night it took the German tourist a long time to fall asleep in his guest room. Thoughts about the rowdy past and the many killings that took place here kept his mind occupied.

8

VISITING THE BIRD CAGE THEATRE

After a hearty cowboy skillet breakfast at the Longhorn Restaurant, Billy walked down to the Bird Cage Theatre. It was around 9:30 a.m. on a weekday, and the town wasn't busy yet. After everything he had read and heard about the famous museum, he felt excited about finally exploring it himself. Billy stood in front of the adobe building on the wooden boardwalk and took a few pictures with his mobile phone. Three tall, arched windows allowed tourists to glimpse into the front area of the museum. One of them was actually a double door which stood wide open, welcoming visitors. Billy entered the Bird Cage and walked toward the bar where he saw a woman readying the cash register for today's business. She wore an Old West outfit. Her black skirt was shorter in front but reached to the heels of her boots on the backside. Her impressive bosom seemed barely controlled by the green satin corset. Net stockings and cowboy boots completed her version of a pioneer saloon girl. Her long hair was piled up in a wild hair style and adorned with colorful feathers. Immediately Billy remembered Magnus's explanation of why this theater was named the Bird Cage and he smiled.

"Howdy Mister. Want to buy a ticket for our beautiful Bird Cage Theatre?"

"Indeed, I do. Is it the self- guided tour?"

"Well, I'll give you some information about the place, then you can roam through the museum all by yourself and take as much time as you wish. The admission is twelve dollars. Are you going to pay with cash or credit card?"

"I'll pay cash." She tore off a blue ticket from her stack and handed him his change. "Oh, before I forget, we also do paranormal investigation tours in the evenings. You might not know, but the Birdcage is supposed to be one of the most haunted locations in the entire US. That ticket would be twenty-five dollars. Think about it, and in case you're interested, I'll add your name on the list for today's evening tour."

"I heard about the place being haunted and will consider that paranormal adventure, but not today," Billy said. After all, he still had more days in Tombstone so there was no need to rush things.

"Well, let's get started on some basic information about this building," she said, stepping in front of the massive hardwood bar. "This front area of the building was the saloon. You see this beautifully hand-carved bar here? It was shipped to Tombstone from thousands of miles away. If I'm not mistaken, it came all the way from the East Coast." She pointed to a railing above the entrance area. "See that gallery up there? When you turn around, you see the stairs leading up to that section. The girls used it to deliver drinks to the gentlemen who occupied the numerous cribs on either side of the building. This ladder-like wood construction next to the bar is something we call the 'booze elevator.' "

Billy chuckled at that expression.

The tour guide went on. "The bartenders filled baskets with bottles and glasses and sent them up the ladder to the gallery where the girls picked the baskets up and delivered the drinks to the guests."

Billy turned around and strolled toward the stairs leading to the second floor of the building. "Is it possible to go up there and have a look at the cribs?"

The lady shook her head. "Unfortunately, not. Due to water

seeping through the roof for many years, we are worried that the floor of the cribs might collapse. We can't risk anyone falling down into the theater room. But once you are in the main section of the place, you will get a pretty good view of those entertainment boxes, as I nickname them."

Billy looked around, studying the different artifacts and the big mechanical music box in the corner. The last song it had played was "Stille Nacht," the German version of "Silent Night."

"I'll be darned. That is the most famous German Christmas song."

The museum employee nodded. "The theater opened December 26, so the owner had this old-style music box imported all the way from Germany. The brass plaque on the front tells the company's name. I reckon a Christmas song fits the season but it sure was never a silent night in here. However, there were many miners of German heritage so they must have felt at home hearing it."

Something felt odd or out of place. He stared at the plywood wall in the welcome area of the Bird Cage. Dozens of pictures and some books were displayed along that wall. A small glass cabinet filled with different minerals stood at the rear. He didn't know why but for some reason the wall appeared fake to him. He'd never been inside the Bird Cage but it seemed to him that patrons should have a direct view of the stage from where he stood. He was confused about his intuition because he didn't know exactly where the stage was located on the other side.

"Was the theater always blocked off from the saloon like this?"

"To be frank, this wall was built only a few years ago. First of all, we needed more space to display all these beautiful pictures, and I reckon the boss-man wanted to prevent people from taking photos of the theater section or getting a free glimpse without paying the admission fee. We have to earn money, right? Folks often fuss about having to pay the entrance fee, but it costs dearly to keep an old structure like this in shape and to make sure future generations are able to enjoy one of the most famous places in the Old West."

That was understandable but Billy was still a bit confused over something. *How did I know that this wall wasn't there in the old days?* Billy wondered. He stared at the stairs leading toward the cribs. "Wow, look at them steps. They are pretty thin in the middle. They are almost worn through. One can only imagine how many men must have walked up and down them."

"Oh, you bet. The first owner named Hutchinson had prostitutes working up there. So, a better view of the show from the theater wasn't the only reason to run up and down those stairs. On a miner's payday, the girls often granted their favors to twenty men or more in one night. Nowadays those steps would likely not hold the weight of people coming in here. The wood is old and brittle, and folks haven't really gotten slimmer compared to the 1880s."

She looked down at her own curvy figure and chuckled. Obviously, the lady had no problem making fun of herself.

"See that door next to the bar? That's where you enter the main museum or theater--whatever you want to call it. All the artifacts in there are silent witnesses of Tombstone's heyday. The original piano still stands in front of the stage. Of course, it is out of tune, and some keys are broken. There are small stairs on the left side of the stage. They will lead you to the area behind it and from there into the downstairs basement where the longest poker game of all the pioneer days took place. It went on as long as the Bird Cage was open. Men had to pay up to a thousand dollars to buy into it. The stakes were incredibly high. Historians estimate that over two million dollars in today's currency changed hands at that poker table. The Bird Cage remained open almost eight and a half years, seven days a week. Historical papers claim it was operating twenty-four hours a day. I'm sure glad they don't have those opening hours any longer."

"So, this place achieved all this fame even though it operated less than ten years?" Billy asked.

"Yes, sir. Don't forget this business offered some wild entertainment. People called it the most notorious honky-tonk between Saint Louis and San Francisco. They had the best performers here on that stage. The highest stakes ever dealt in poker games in the entire West changed hands here. And let's not forget the girls of the red-light district. Tombstone had an unbelievable number of prostitutes and some of them are still famous to this day. Those women conquered the West as much as any soldier, prospector, or gunfighter did."

Billy listened to the lady, fascinated by her knowledge. As she mentioned the soiled doves of Tombstone, a sudden sadness hit him as if somebody kicked him in the gut. A memory crossed his mind, but it was gone as quickly as it came. Before he was able to grab it, the feeling vanished into his subconscious again. Billy shook his head, then he thanked her and walked through the side door, leaving the saloon area behind. He was ready to explore the theater and the Bird Cage was ready to welcome him.

9

WHISPERING VOICES

Billy stepped into the Bird Cage's surprisingly dark main room. After a few moments, his eyes adjusted to the dimly lit area. Billy would never have thought that the inside of the theater was so spacious because the building didn't appear this big from the outside. It must have held hundreds of guests during its heydays.

He remained standing in the corner next to the doorway and glanced upward toward the ceiling where the cribs were arrayed. They looked very much like historical cinema niches. Faded red velvet curtains flanked each of them. In two of the cribs, the museum owners had placed mannequins dressed up as historical gunfighters. They stared at him as if he were an intruder.

Billy advanced slowly into the room, glancing around him. Although he knew it was ridiculous, he had the feeling that the eyes of the mannequins followed him. Paintings of circus scenes protected by thick glass adorned the walls underneath the cribs. The passage of many years had yellowed the canvases. From the books Billy had read, he knew that traveling circuses performed in the pioneer towns, so the pictures didn't strike him as odd.

The entire room was full of artifacts displayed in glass cabinets along the walls and on huge tables in the center. It was a motley collection and didn't follow a system like most museum exhibitions.

Billy strolled along the wall opposite the entry door. Now he understood why the additional plywood had been added to separate the saloon section from this big room. It provided enough space for numerous Winchesters and pictures from the old days to be hung almost all the way to the high ceiling.

As Billy studied his surroundings, he understood that the occupants of the saloon in the old days had a clear view all the way to the stage, just as he had assumed. They would have been able to watch the people drinking and flirting at the tables and the cancan dancers on the stage. *Wait a minute,* cancan *dancers? How in the world would you know that there were girls dancing that French extravaganza that even inspired some ballets?* Billy shrugged his shoulders. *Must have read it somewhere*, he thought.

He passed one of the big tables and almost stumbled over a pile of baskets. "The beverage baskets," he whispered. But how could he know? Billy walked toward the stage and in his head, he heard piano music and loud cheering. He wheeled around to stare at the walls and ceiling, trying to find the music speakers producing the sound. Perhaps walking through the room had activated the musical entertainment. It was a neat trick and added to the atmosphere. But he couldn't see any speakers. *Maybe they installed them in the cribs, hiding them from the visitors*, Billy assumed.

The stage was big enough to provide space for ten or more dancers whirling in frenzied dance. Long velvet curtains hung sadly from the high ceiling. Their once ruby-red color was now a faded maroon with dusty, golden fringes. When he gazed upwards, he saw countless bullet holes in the ceiling, and water stains from decades of rain finding its way into the building marred the white paint above him. Billy could still find no explanation where the music came from, but he could still hear the old-fashioned polka loud and clear. And he heard something else...

A female voice whispered, repeatedly calling the name "William." Billy was sure that some other visitors to the museum must be following him or could be downstairs in the other section of the building. No wonder he heard voices. He shook his head and grinned.

He walked from display to display and marveled at all the artifacts. There were household items and dishes made from pure silver. Billy wondered if ore from Tombstone had been used to produce them. One section held old typewriters, musical instruments, and a big iron safe. It looked sturdy enough to survive a blast from a stick of dynamite. There was gambling equipment, faro and poker tables, and an extensive collection of guns—old Winchesters, which Billy loved and Colt six-shooters of every caliber.

Billy walked past the piano and the stage to a small flight of stairs next to the faded velvet curtain. The steps took him to the backstage area, which wasn't big. The walls to the left were covered with promotional prints announcing certain entertainers of the old days and a glass cabinet displaying a woman's clothes.

"How tiny she must have been," he mumbled. The waist on the dress could be encircled by his two hands. The funeral hearse Magnus told him about dominated the entire backstage room.

The German tourist took a few pictures of the Black Moriah, then studied the fine craftsmanship. A sign next to it claimed the owner's insurance company appraised the hearse as worth an unbelievable two million dollars.

Billy whistled through his teeth. *Must be some idealized worth that considers the history of the people who were transported to Boot Hill in it,* he mused. Billy wondered how much the owner's grandparents paid for the entire museum with all its items inside. *They probably got it mighty cheap. After all, the place was closed and the locale was little more than a ghost town when the Hunley family took it over. Who would have thought that this building would be such a gold mine once Tombstone opened its history to paying tourists a couple of decades later?*

Billy felt a twinge of envy for the family who owns this precious piece of history. Looking at the adobe walls now protected against tourist hands by nets of wire mesh, Billy couldn't help but wonder how much longer the building could withstand the elements of rain, wind, and summer heat. People told him that the weather could be pretty severe in Cochise County--especially the monsoon storms were a force to be reckoned with.

"William, come to me." There it was again, a young woman's voice, sweet and plaintive, but he couldn't see the woman.

Confused, Billy shook his head and walked toward the stairs leading to the basement. "That must be the gambling area where that epic poker game took place," he whispered. To his surprise no other visitors were down there. *Where in the world did that voice come from? It sure sounded pleasant.*

Billy leaned against the banister separating two prostitution chambers from the poker area. Strangely the table looked as if the players got up barely a few minutes ago. Crumpled dollar bills and old poker chips Covered the faded green felt surface of the gambling table. Coins from all over the world lay on the table as well as on the dirt floor. For some reason the hardwood floor which covered most of the basement had never been finished under that poker table. Billy made a mental note to ask his new friend Magnus about it. The playing cards were yellowed with age, but Billy recognized them as the same sort they used in Germany.

He took a few pictures and glanced into the two rooms with the antique furniture in them. According to the sign, these rooms were reserved for the high-priced fallen angels. Billy felt a tingle of excitement as he stared at one of the iron beds. Although the thought of people witnessing what was going on behind those doors was disgusting to him, and he would have never considered spending a night with a prostitute, he still felt drawn to the second chamber.

He glanced at the full-length dressing mirror and the old, faded rug on the floor. Moths had chewed countless holes into the quilt covering the old bed. A potbellied stove must have offered a fair amount of warmth in the old days. A lace nightgown hung from a hook next to the antique dressing mirror. A silver hairbrush on top of the bureau made Billy imagine one of the soiled doves brushing her long hair.

The air smelled dusty down here, and the entire building

confused the young man, although he couldn't put a finger on why. He turned and studied the gambling area with the makeshift bar at its back once again. A smaller table next to the bar held another gambling gadget that resembled a cage shaped like an hourglass. He wondered if this corner was where Chuck-a-luck had been played. Billy frowned. *Who the hell told me about Chuck-a-luck? For Christ's sake, I don't even know the German word for this game or the rules for it.*

10

OPTICAL ILLUSIONS

"William. Mi Corazón. ¡Me lo prometiste!"

"Who is there? My name is not William, and I don't speak Spanish." Yet he understood what the voice said. "My darling, you promised me." Who spoke to him from some shadowy corner of this long-forgotten gambling place? What promise was the voice talking about?

Billy stared at the poker table, and his nose caught the scent of a sweet iron-like smell. To his amazement the green, dusty velvet beneath the bills and poker chips turned crimson. The stain hadn't been there before. His eyes grew big when it seemed to spread even further, and the trickling of drops filled his ears, although he heard no other sounds. He stared at the table and saw a thick, red liquid flowing over the table's edge and collecting in a puddle on the dirt floor where it seeped into the ground. *Good heavens, this looks like blood.*

Billy stumbled into the adjoining room full of historic framed photos and documents. His stomach felt queasy, and he walked briskly through the small gift store. He had no interest in the countless souvenirs for sale. All he wanted was to step through the side exit and out into the fresh air.

Billy shook his head in disbelief. The glaring morning sun blinded him for a few moments. He walked around the building back to the front entrance. The lady at the cash register looked up from her mobile phone and smiled at him. "Hey there, did you enjoy the tour?"

Billy tried to catch his breath. "There's something wrong down there in the poker area. The table--there's a lot of blood on it, and I'm sure someone must have gotten hurt. I heard the voice of a woman who might be hiding somewhere inside one of the rooms. I couldn't find her but I believe she is injured. Good grief, you need to come and check out all the blood. Something bad must have happened in the basement."

To Billy's surprise the lady remained calm and didn't rise from behind the register. "I'll check it out later. Thanks for letting me know though."

He couldn't believe his ears. Billy stared at the woman and wondered if she hadn't understood his accent. She didn't seem to be the least bit alarmed about him telling a wild tale of their table being full of blood. Either she didn't get what he was saying, or she didn't believe him.

He tried again. "Listen lady, I saw a hell of a lot of blood down there, and I heard the woman calling out, but she's nowhere to be seen. I don't know if she left the museum already, but something happened in that basement. Before all your visitors have the shock of their lives, you had better have a look at that mess. By the amount of blood, I'm sure that someone urgently needs help."

"Mister, I don't doubt that you have seen something strange. To be honest it happens all the time, but I have to admit that seeing blood is a new thing. Why do you think we do paranormal tours in the evenings? The Bird Cage is an eerie place from time to time, and some events that happen here can't be explained. Did you take any pictures of the blood by any chance?"

Billy shook his head, but he knew what he saw. The iron-like smell still lingered in his nostrils. He reflected on her words and her calm demeanor. Could it have been an optical illusion? Did he really see the stain? Did he hear that Spanish-speaking woman? Billy was so confused he turned around and walked out of the Bird Cage Theatre without saying goodbye to the woman behind the bar. He didn't look back. If he had, he would have caught her worried expression. Her eyes showed fear.

Billy crossed the street and walked straight into the Oriental Saloon. Despite the fact that it was before lunch time he ordered a shot of whiskey. He recalled how he had become dizzy in the Courthouse Museum and now this. *What in the world is wrong with you, Hoss*?

He spent the rest of the day strolling through town, but he didn't pay attention to the stores and shows. Billy called it a day early and went back to the San Jose House. Rather than eating out, he ordered some takeaway food, which he ate at the dining table. He and Magnus intended to ride out to some of the sights outside Tombstone the following day.

His sleep was haunted by a beautiful Mexican girl who pointed an accusing finger at him constantly saying, "You promised, me Corazón, you promised and you lied."

Billy tossed and turned in his bed and finally gave up on sleep. He got up before dawn lit the sky, brewed some coffee, and sat on the porch of his room enjoying the sunrise. However, the woman he saw in his dream occupied his thoughts for most of the morning.

11

THE GHOST TOWN TRAIL

Magnus arrived around ten o'clock. He rode a BMW with a sidecar, occupied by his black dog Chaco. Billy went over to the dog and scratched him behind his ears. Chaco was a friendly animal and showed his enthusiasm for the trip by frolicking around his owner's bike.

"You know I find it kind of funny that you as a German ride an American bike and me as an American, bought a German BMW."

Billy laughed and handed Magnus a cup of steaming coffee. "So where are we going today?" he wanted to know.

"I thought we'd have a look-see at some of the Ghost Trail towns. Gleeson will be our first stop. They remodeled the prison there. It's a neat building. Parts of the schoolhouse also still exist, although most of it burned down decades ago. Then we'll ride to the other side of the Stronghold Canyon. That's the rugged terrain you see on the left-hand side when entering Tombstone from St. David. That canyon is famous because it was the hiding place for Geronimo, Cochise, and other famous chiefs. Cochise even established his reservation on its east side. The Apache reverence the Dragoon Mountains and the Stronghold Canyon as sacred land."

"I'm looking forward to seeing Stronghold Canyon that I've read about."

Magnus explained the rest of his plans for the day. "We'll have a lunch stop at that famous Fort Bowie where they captured Geronimo before deporting him to Florida. There's a neat little museum. It's a short hike from the parking lot, but the area is beautiful. On the way back we'll stop at a town called Bisbee. It was a thriving copper mining community. Nowadays it's a cool little hippie town with numerous galleries and secondhand stores. We can have dinner at the Copper Queen Hotel. It's as old as the town itself and they have great food. We should be back in Tombstone before it gets too dark."

"Sounds like an exciting day," Billy said and carried the two mugs back into the guestroom. He locked the door and both men prepared to ride their bikes out of town. It was a beautiful, sunny day with ideal temperatures for exploring the area by motorcycle. Billy enjoyed the company of his new friend who was able to explain about the different settlements in Cochise County.

Around two o'clock in the afternoon they arrived at Fort Bowie on the other side of the Dragoon Mountains. It lay nestled in a side canyon with red rocks around it on an open field covered with foxtail grass and mesquite trees. Some of the structures were well-kept, and the sheltered exhibit informed visitors about the history of this military outpost. An impressive cannon sat on the porch of the officer's headquarters which hosted the museum.

"You know, when Geronimo surrendered, he was kept prisoner here for a couple of days before they were able to deport him and his remaining band," Magnus explained. "See that cemetery behind those adobe walls? Not only soldiers are buried there but also one of Geronimo's children. His infant son named *Little Robe* died here in this fort."

The two men walked over and paid their respect to the grave. Billy couldn't help but wonder how devastated Geronimo's family must have felt losing beloved family members and being forced to give up their freedom for good just to survive. As a German, the topic of genocide and the shame it triggered in following generations was familiar to Billy.

"There were many wrongdoings on both sides during the Indian wars I think," Billy said. Magnus nodded. "Way too many people lost their lives because of hatred, greed, and racism. It is a terrible wound which may never heal."

Magnus and Billy sat down at the compact picnic area and unpacked the sandwiches they bought on the way. Nowadays, it appeared to be a peaceful place, yet one could sense the tragic history and the bloody past of the Apache wars that took place in the surrounding canyons.

Magnus studied Billy's face. He took a long sip of his cold Coke before he spoke. "So, did you pay a visit to the Bird Cage yesterday?" he wanted to know.

Billy nodded. "Sure did. Amazing place. I understand why people in town call it a must-see."

"It sure is impressive," Magnus replied. "But tell me my friend, you seem to be serious today and not as cheerful as you were the other day in the saloon. Are you alright?"

Billy chewed as if he needed time to think about what he was going to say next. "You are a very observant person, Magnus. Oh, what the hell, might as well spill the beans. I reckon that if there's one person I can talk to about what I saw yesterday, it is you. It started with me recognizing that an extra plywood wall wasn't there in the old days, but there was no way I could have known that. The sudden thought that the audience couldn't have seen the cancan dancers on stage if that wall had existed in the 1880s crossed my mind. You know, I'm referring to the one which separates the entrance area where the bar is from the rest of the building. Now how in the world would I know what dances were featured? I mean, the cancan was a Paris thing, but surely not one you would expect in Tombstone, Arizona in the middle of the frontier. But I'm hundred percent sure that it was performed at that theater. I mean, I even heard the piano music and the cheers of the crowd. At first, I was pretty sure that my imagination was running wild with all the things I've heard about the place."

"At first?" Magnus asked. "That sounds as if you changed your opinion about it. What happened?"

Billy laughed but it was a nervous sound and had an undertone of fear that he couldn't hide from his friend. "I know this will probably sound completely ridiculous, and I'm not even sure if I really saw the things down in the basement."

Magnus shook his head and opened another soda. He passed it to Billy before taking one for himself out of the saddlebag. "Believe me, in all the years I have lived in Tombstone, nothing sounds ridiculous to me anymore. It's pretty obvious something scared you down there."

"I heard the voice. It was the voice of a woman speaking Spanish. She called out for someone named William, and she sounded accusing and sad. I don't speak Spanish but she called this William 'Corazón' and constantly repeated a word that sounded like 'promise.' I'm not sure to whom she was talking. The weird part is that there weren't any female visitors in the museum at the time, but I heard her voice loud and clear."

Magnus scratched his chin. "Hmm, corazón means 'darling,' and if the other words sounded something similar to 'promedito' it is indeed the Mexican word for promised. The voice might have called you because Billy is the short form of William. It's absolutely possible that one of the Bird Cage inhabitants spoke to you. People hear voices in that building all the time, even if there are no visitors around."

Billy frowned thoughtfully, "I sure wished I had only heard the voice," he mumbled. "What do you mean?" Magnus asked.

Taking a deep breath, Billy went on. "I looked at the poker table and... Jesus, how am I going to say this? I mean, I probably sound like a nutcase."

Magnus waited patiently. It was obvious that something had frightened his German friend inside the museum. He seemed nervous and reluctant to speak.

"When I first looked at the poker table, all I saw was the money there, coins, notes and of course, countless poker chips. But after the woman whispered to me again, I turned around, and there was a stain on that table. It had the crimson color of blood, and I saw liquid dripping onto the floor. For Christ's sake, I even heard the drops falling. I'm sure it was blood, and it seeped into the ground under the poker table. For whatever reason, that area is dirt floor and it soaked up what was dripping from that piece of furniture."

Magnus stared at his friend. "Wow, I'll be darned. No wonder you are lost in thought today. You know the poker game had already started, so the carpenter wasn't allowed to finish the hardwood floor as none of the players were willing to interrupt the game. And you think it was really blood you saw?"

"To be frank, I don't know what to think but there was that smell, a sweet iron-like smell so yes, I'm sure it was blood. I went back to the entrance and told the lady about it, but believe it or not, she didn't even bother to walk down the stairs and check on what I was reporting. She more or less behaved pretty unconcerned about it."

"The employees there are used to weird things happening so yes, it might have been lack of concern or maybe even fear. However, something about this story bugs me. That image of blood on the poker table rings a bell, but I can't recall it. Give me a day or two, and I'll check my diary. I'm sure I wrote something down about events and killings happening at the Bird Cage during its heyday."

"You keep a diary?"

"Yes. I started it about six months after coming here. I came across so much history and so many eerie tales that I was afraid I would start to forget things after a while. So, I went to the department store and bought me a couple of notebooks. Whenever I find some solid proof for another piece of history of this town, I write it into those diaries. That includes all the paranormal stuff visitors and locals experience in Tombstone and tell me about. I have been able to collect some of the tragedies that occurred inside the Bird Cage and other famous buildings around here. As I said, there's something about that poker table that I must have heard, but it might have been in the first year after I moved here. Otherwise, I would remember better. Boy, we are all getting older, aren't we? Anyway, the reason why I write all that stuff down is that I eventually plan to write a book with a historian named Ben Traywick. He is an older fellow and lives in town. Ben knows a lot about the early days of Tombstone. Sadly, he hasn't been in the best shape lately."

"I would really appreciate it if you could find out if there was any event in connection with that poker table. I didn't sleep well last night and dreamed about a beautiful Mexican shady lady, but the woman in my dream constantly accused me of something. I'm not sure what it was, but the dream seemed very realistic. Normally I'm not the kind of man that has dreams or remembers them the following morning. I know it sounds crazy, but she was familiar to me, although I can't place where I would have met her. I don't know any Spanish or Mexican women."

"You know, many people tell me that their dreams are so realistic, sometimes it's as if a person visits them. As a matter of fact, when you sleep your consciousness is shut off. Some people believe that it is then easier for spirits to visit when our rationally thinking consciousness is not getting into their way. Society questions and even denies the existence of ghosts or spirits, as some call them. I don't question them. God knows, I have seen things that aren't explainable with science--things that could scare a man to death. My guess is you have some sort of connection to the Bird Cage, and that the woman in your dream might be a person who lived in a long-forgotten time. If that is the case it means that you have lived here during a former lifetime. I don't expect you to believe any of this but I know what I have experienced here. Sometimes people come here and get confronted with unfinished business of yesteryear if you understand what I mean."

Billy shrugged his shoulders. "But all those people of the 1880s, they are dead and gone. Why would they still think that they have unfinished business if their entire life is over?"

12

DO SPIRITS LINGER?

Magnus' face turned serious. He spoke softly, almost as if he expected that some of yesterday's pioneers could be listening to what he had to say about them. "Billy, I don't believe that they are aware that their life is over. A lot of people in Tombstone were killed in the blink of an eye. The town was rowdy and at times, brutal. Dying people often had no time to prepare for death. I think it's possible that they continue living their life of the old days in some sort of parallel dimension to our modern days without being aware that times have moved on. There are some places in this world that are like an open portal, and my personal belief is that these gateways offer a possibility for spirits to pass from one time period to another century."

"Jesus, are you telling me you think it's like a time traveling deal?"

Magnus shook his head. "Not really, at least not in the science fiction sense. People think that time traveling would allow modern-day mankind to travel either back in the past or into the future. The portals I'm talking about are meant for the spirits to be able to travel back to the time when they lived their lives. However, people who are alive nowadays can't travel into the life of the spirits because for us modern folks, it's the past which we consider to be gone. So, it is like a one-way track. We can't pass these portals because our bodies aren't compatible with them."

"That sounds impossible. Those centuries are gone for good."

"For us they are," Magnus said. "But possibly not for the spirits. When I worked as tour guide in one of the Tombstone mines, I swear to God, I saw the shadows of miners still chiseling away and heard the constant metallic clink, clink, clink of their hammers hitting those metal chisels. They are still searching for that damn silver that destroyed their lives because some of them simply don't get it that they are dead--that they missed the moment when they should have gone into the light."

"But wouldn't that be terrible? That would mean that those souls are prisoners on this plane of existence."

Magnus nodded. "Billy, I believe some of these townspeople were truly cursed. We speak about hell as eternal damnation. What if these spirits are stuck in a former life like an endless loop with no escape and no chance to find peace for their poor soul? What if that eternal damnation happens right here on earth? Imagine how confusing it must be for them to see a modern-day Tombstone with motorized vehicles, electricity, and other modern amenities. One thing seems certain, they recognize souls that were part of their life in the old days, and they seek those souls as if they could gain energy from them. It might be like bringing part of the old days back to them."

"Holy cow, I never saw life from that point of view. I mean I have heard that certain places in this world are supposed to be haunted, but what you are saying makes sense. That scares me."

Magnus packed up the waste and the empty coke cans. "Enough talk about the dead for the moment. It is a somber topic for such a fine day. Let's ride to Bisbee, my friend. It's a neat place and full of true history as well. I'll check those diaries tomorrow, and we can meet for dinner. If I find anything that seems connected to what you saw down there in the gambling area, I'll let you know immediately."

"I really appreciate it. Thanks for listening without judging."

"You're welcome. I'm grateful for the opportunity to meet you in person and find a good friend."

They spent the rest of the day in the copper mining community of Bisbee. Chaco enjoyed the stroll along the streets, and Magnus pampered him with a little ice cream which he eagerly licked out of the small cup.

"Where did you get Chaco?" Billy asked while watching the dog enjoying his sweet treat.

"That was another mystery of life. I traveled through the Northern part of Arizona with my dog Ripples. We explored the area around Chaco Canyon. For whatever reason Ripples got very sick. I stayed in the closest town, and the vet fought for that poor soul for three days. Cost me my entire travel budget for the next two months but in the end, I had to ask the vet to put him down. Ripples was like a family member to me. Heartbroken, I drove to the native American dwellings of Chaco Canyon. Believe it or not, that evening a dark dog walked into my camp. I have no clue where he came from because nobody lives out there. Since there was nobody around camping but me, I reckoned he was a stray. I asked around in town the following day, but nobody knew Chaco. It almost seemed as if the spirit of Ripples sent him when I most needed him. We left Chaco Canyon together, and he has been by my side ever since. He's a good boy."

"Wow, now I know where he got his name. That is indeed a unique story. You might be right that destiny sent a replacement to help you cope with the loss of Ripples. I doubt that this was a coincidence. I'm sure you two were meant to meet."

Magnus nodded and petted the big, black dog. "I totally agree with you. Chaco and I are meant to be companions. Animals are often the better people anyway."

It was after sunset when Billy arrived back at the San Jose House. He was tired and decided to call it a day without going into town. There were some leftovers from last night's dinner in the fridge, and he warmed them up and took a shower.

His thoughts turned back to the conversation he had with Magnus at Fort Bowie. Despite the fact that he was brought up in a world where science was able to explain almost everything, Billy still had the feeling that there might be a lot of truth in what Magnus said about the world of spirits.

Billy's night was again restless. Images of the beautiful Mexican girl had him tossing and turning in bed. She was a looker, all right, and he would have felt drawn to her if she was a real person. This time he saw her face more clearly. Her eyes were wide and dark as a moonless night. Her eyelashes were the longest he had ever seen, and the delicately arched brows created the perfect frame for her eyes. Her mouth was full and very kissable. The color of her lips was so dark it seemed as though she might be wearing lipstick, but women didn't have easy access to cosmetics in those days. It must be her natural shade. Billy didn't know. All he knew was that he was yearning to kiss them. Her figure was slim, the waist emphasized with a corset. She wore a blouse which left her shoulders bare, and he could clearly see the curve of her full bosom.

Billy broke out in a sweat and kicked his bed covers all the way down to his feet. The woman in his dream smiled at him, yet her eyes looked so sad. He didn't know what was wrong, but somehow, he couldn't deny the feeling that he was responsible for her sadness.

When Billy woke up the following morning, he felt exhausted. As he brewed his coffee, strangely he could remember every detail of his dream. Billy couldn't recall ever having felt so confused in his entire life. And there was something else--he couldn't remember feeling so emotionally touched by any woman, not even his ex-wife.

13

THE GRAVE

After a hearty breakfast of scrambled eggs, bacon, and a side of fresh English muffins at the O.K. Cafe opposite the Four Deuces Saloon, Billy decided to do more sightseeing in town. He remembered riding past the sign announcing Boot Hill Cemetery when he rode into town the first day. The athletic man didn't need his motorcycle but walked the short distance. Unlike most tourists, he didn't mind walking and enjoyed it. He strolled through the small gift shop and stepped outside, taking the rear exit into the open cemetery. Most graves were unadorned piles of dirt and rocks. Ocotillos and cacti grew between them. Each grave was marked with a wooden marker announcing the name and quite often the cause of death of the person buried beneath it.

Of course, Billy was looking for the ones where the victims of the O.K. Corral gunfight found their last rest. He tried to imagine how those boys were brought here in the Black Moriah funeral hearse he had seen at the Bird Cage Theatre two days ago. As he walked along the gravel paths, he studied each of the markers.

He planned to read more about Tombstone and its glory days, aware that some of the names sounded familiar to him, and he wanted to know more about their lives. He saw a burial site of a woman called China Mary. She must have been an important person in this town because her grave was somewhat decorated with an iron fence around it.

It didn't take long before he found the graves of the brothers Tom and Frank McLaury and Billy Clanton. Their grave markers informed visitors that all three men were murdered in the streets of Tombstone. Billy knew that there was an ongoing discussion about whether the Earps murdered those boys in cold blood, or the gang of cowboys provoked justice to be brought upon them.

Billy strolled from grave to grave, taking a picture now and then. He wondered about the destinies of the people behind those names. One marker stated the man had been dragged by a rope into the open grave because he died of pox. Nobody wanted to touch the body for fear of catching the disease, not even the undertakers.

"What a sad way to get buried, pulled into a dug-out hole like a dead animal," Billy mumbled.

A mob lynched another victim of the roughness of the times after he committed a crime in Bisbee. A posse must have caught him in Tombstone and didn't waste time on a trial but hung him right away. Some tombstones even had short poems painted on them, like the one about a cowboy who ended up with four slugs in his body.

"My oh my, people are surely not exaggerating when they say that Tombstone had a man for breakfast every single day," Billy mumbled and took a sip from his water bottle.

There was only one small section remaining, and he walked over to it. A square marker, low to the ground, stood over one grave. It looked like it had been recently replaced. The wood hadn't yet been weathered by the torching summer sun, and it was much shorter than all the others. *Maybe it is that of a child,* Billy mused.

He walked toward it. A cross was painted on the board. There was no family name given. It simply read as Margarita--stabbed by Gold Dollar.

Billy felt as if somebody kicked him in the gut. He stared at Margarita's grave and felt like throwing up. A grief he had never experienced before clutched his heart. He wasn't aware that he held his breath until he tried to choke back tears and tasted bitter bile.

"What in the world is the matter with you?" he scolded himself. "It's only an old grave. Nothing more than a pile of rocks and probably some bones underneath, if these people are really buried at this very spot, that is."

He felt ashamed of the tears he wiped away. Billy hoped that no one saw him crying. He had no rational explanation for why this grave marker touched him so deeply, but seeing the name Margarita saddened him. She had been stabbed by Gold Dollar. Who was Gold Dollar? Was it a man or a woman? Did the female inhabitants in Tombstone's past kill each other?

Billy stood unmoving, incapable of taking his eyes off the painted board. It seemed to be glaring back at him accusingly. Billy didn't know how long he stood there. He lost track of time and didn't pay attention to the people who stared at him as they passed. When he finally turned and left Boot Hill, he totally forgot to buy one of the printed brochures explaining each grave.

As he walked through the front gate of the cemetery, his phone rang. He answered it absently. It was Magnus. "Howdy my friend, I'm going to town this evening to enjoy the special at the Longhorn. It's baby back ribs today. You should try them. They're delicious."

"Sounds good to me. I need to talk to you about something, anyway. How about we meet at six o'clock in front of the restaurant?"

"Excellent. See you there at sixish." Billy tucked the phone back into his hip pocket. He was confused but knew he needed to find out more about Margarita and Gold Dollar. Thinking of the names gave him the chills and he didn't know why seeing that particular grave affected him so intensely.

14

MURDER STORIES

The two friends met in front of the restaurant. They ordered the special and waited for their beverages. The smell inside the Longhorn was mouthwatering, and Billy realized that he had not eaten since breakfast.

"What did you do today?" Magnus asked.

"Went to that Boot Hill Cemetery."

Magnus grinned. "Doing the touristy thing, are you?"

Billy shrugged. "Are the people mentioned on those grave markers really buried there?"

Magnus thought for a moment. "Kind of. They had to move some of the graves when they built those two roads around the cemetery. and the folks might not be buried exactly where the grave markers are. Originally, that piece of land was given to the town by one of the founding families named Escapule from France. According to some town documents, most of the characters really existed and are six feet below the surface of Boot Hill. but for some folks mentioned, there is no proof that they lived in Tombstone, nor any proof they are buried at Boot Hill Cemetery."

Billy smiled grimly. "I wondered about that."

"Not everything in this town is authentic. Sadly, a lot of history got watered down for the sake of tourist dollars. Tombstone was almost done and falling apart after the silver rush ended. In the early 1920s, this settlement was little more than a ghost town, so the remaining inhabitants had to do something to attract visitors. Not always for the best, if you ask me, but it was a matter of survival for those who stayed here after the silver rush. I think the first touristy event they ever did was a Helldorado Festival with a parade in 1929. It was a special occasion honoring the fiftieth anniversary of the founding of the town with thirty groups of reenactors, dancers, and music. They also reenacted the famous gunfight at the O.K. Corral. Helldorado Days have taken place every October since then."

Their food arrived and both men enjoyed their barbecued ribs in silence. When they finished eating, Billy asked, "Is it true that more than fifteen thousand people lived here during the boom years?"

Magnus shook his head. "Likely many more, because only the white men who owned property were counted in the census. Imagine--all the Chinese, Mexicans, married women, and shady ladies were not even included. My guess is the population was over twenty-five thousand people."

The waitress brought coffee after clearing their empty plates. Billy stirred his cup thoughtfully. "Have the mines completely run out of silver, and that triggered the decision to close them?"

"No. In fact, there is still silver in them hills, but the rising ground water made mining extremely difficult. New silver strikes and the US government no longer purchasing silver caused prices to hit rock bottom in the 1890s. Mining became only a quarter as profitable as it had been before."

Magnus said then pulled a small notebook from his jacket. "To change the subject, I did a bit of reading and found some information about the deaths which occurred in the Bird Cage. As I mentioned before, it is said that twenty-six people died inside that building one way or the other. Most got shot or stabbed over a lousy deck of cards or fighting over a soiled dove. I reckon most folks must have been under the influence of alcohol or perhaps opium, and their tempers had a short fuse. I also found out that one of the dancers died when the rope on a sandbag used to lower the big curtain snapped, and the bag came crashing down backstage onto the poor girl's head. She must have crossed the stage area at the wrong moment, and didn't have the slightest chance of survival."

Billy stared at his friend. Twenty-six people. No wonder the building gave him the chills.

"There was a couple who committed suicide in one of the prostitution chambers downstairs. They packed a lot of coal in the potbellied stove and died of carbon monoxide poisoning. It is said they were madly in love, but he couldn't afford to pay Hutchinson, the owner at the time, enough to free his soiled dove darling. Since they couldn't marry and start a family they decided to at least die together."

"Sweet Mary in heaven, how tragic. This is terrible. But where did you get all this information?"

Magnus smiled. "Best way to do research is reading old newspapers, my friend. I went through their archives and searched some museum papers as well. Of course, some articles are exaggerated but they contain a lot of true stories and were printed in the days when these events occurred."

Billy swallowed nervously. "Have you found out if any gamblers killed each other down in the basement?"

Magnus shook his head. "In the main theater room, they actually did. One fellow got shot over a faro game and one army officer from Fort Huachuca was assassinated through the entrance door for being friends with the law dogs, but nothing down there where you've seen the blood."

After a moment of silence, Billy cleared his throat. "You know, one of the graves at this Boot Hill place really shook me up today."

Magnus frowned. "Probably the McLaury and Clanton grave, is it? Some people still claim that it was cold-blooded murder at the O.K. Corral. It has been an ongoing discussion for decades. Some say the boys were unarmed and unable to defend themselves against the Earps. Others claim that the Earps shot in self-defense as the McLaurys and Clanton opened fire against them."

Billy shook his head. "Actually, it was a grave in a different section with only a small marker. One 'Margarita' is supposed to be buried there. It seems she got stabbed by some Gold Dollar fellow. I don't know why, but it shook me up to see the place. Actually, it made me cry like some dang soap opera fool."

Magnus stared at him without saying a word. Then he frowned, caught up in his own thoughts. The constant noise of the other guests annoyed Billy. When Magnus spoke, it made Billy jump. "Oh, my God, is it really possible?"

Billy looked confused. "What? What is it?"

"I recall a story about those days that can cast some light on what you experienced. Would you mind going back to your rooms at the San Jose House and talk there in more private surroundings?" Magnus asked.

Billy nodded. Both men paid for their meals then walked over to Fremont Street. Billy brewed some fresh coffee.

"We will have to do more research. I'll talk to a friend of mine who works at the Courthouse Museum. I hope we can get access to the trial documents of 1882 that contain the information we need."

Billy frowned. "What are we looking for?"

Magnus stirred sugar into his steaming beverage. He seemed to ponder how to tell Billy his suspicions about why Margarita's grave had troubled his German friend.

When Magnus finally spoke, he wore a serious expression. "As you know a lot of gambling was going on in the Birdcage in the old days. Some gamblers were professionals--folks like Russian Bill, Doc Holliday, and others. Among them was a guy named William Milgreen, nicknamed Billy. Like most gamblers, he had a common-law wife. Those women were mostly prostitutes. Wyatt Earp was involved with one and so was his brother. Women willing to live with a man and take care of him without being married were rare. Some wives or s of those famous characters even ran their own brothels."

Billy nodded and drank his coffee. Billy Milgreen. Same first name. *Weird coincidence*, he thought.

Magnus continued. “Milgreen was involved with a woman named Gold Dollar.”

Billy stared at Magnus, eyes huge with surprise. “My goodness, that’s the name on the grave marker.”

Magnus nodded. “Gold Dollar worked at the Crystal Palace Saloon. I’m not sure if she charged a gold dollar for her favors, as she was one of the fallen angels, or if the name referred to her golden blond hair. During that specific year, a new sort of gold dollar was coined in the US, so I would think it was rather what she charged for her temporary female affection.”

“Wait, she was a prostitute, you say?”

Magnus shrugged his shoulders. “A lot of women were. Historians think that over a thousand prostitutes plied their trade here. This town was busy and made a lot of money. Sure different compared to nowadays,” he added with a chuckle.

The two men laughed and Billy refilled the coffee cups. He liked this man a lot. Talking to Magnus was like stepping back in time to the glory days of Tombstone. He hadn’t admitted it to anybody, but for some reason, he felt at home here despite the weird things happening around him. Billy even considered extending his stay in Tombstone.

“Where was I? Oh, yeah, Miss Gold Dollar. It is said that she used to perform as a dancer at the Bird Cage before moving on to the Crystal Palace saloon. During her days at the Bird Cage Theatre, she called herself Little Gertie. Now you as a German surely know that it stands for Gertrude. No wonder because she was of German heritage. Gold Dollar was said to be short in stature, and I assume that’s where her name “Little Gertie" came from. Despite her short legs she was said to have been a feisty little devil and a great dancer. I bet the Bird Cage was the place where she got to know Billy Milgreen.”

“Makes sense if she was performing there and he was one of the regular gamblers on that premises,” Billy agreed. “But how does Margarita fit into that story?”

“Old newspapers claim that new girls arrived in town almost every day, just like thousands of miners. They came by stagecoach and some of the madams running brothels always made sure there was fresh flesh in their houses of ill repute. They even had a French syndicate which imported furniture, dresses, silk stockings, and champaign for their brothels. In those days, Tombstone had a taste for luxury, and folks were decadent because they could afford it. The miners and the women of easy morals had one thing in common--they were soldiers of fortune looking for a way to earn enough money for a better tomorrow. Women were highly outnumbered along the entire frontier, so towns like Tombstone demanded fresh female blood all the time. The high-class prostitutes earned a fortune, but they often caught syphilis or got old and unattractive. Some had too many children to feed and many were laudanum addicted or committed suicide. Therefore, the demand for new women never ceased."

Billy took a sip of his coffee. "Wow, Tombstone sounds like a mixture between Sodom and Hollywood."

Magnus laughed. "You got that right, my friend. Well, little Gertie and Milgreen were getting along well. Her steady income as a fallen angel provided him with enough money to follow his passion as a poker player. He was addicted to gambling, and some nights, he would win a lot of money, but other nights Gertie would make more cash than he could have ever won at the poker tables. I'm sure she was dreaming of marrying him and starting a family in the near future, though I doubt he had the same plans."

Billy raised his hand to stop his friend. "Magnus, there's one thing I don't understand. You told me that she was a prostitute. Why should she have reason to kill another woman? Surely not out of jealousy because she was seeing other men every night, I assume. Wouldn't he have the same right to do so?"

"You're right about that, but believe it or not, she was really jealous. She considered sleeping with her johns as part of her employment, but I'm sure that she was in love with Billy Milgreen in a mighty possessive way. It worked for them until the day when the tall, dark beauty named Margarita came into town. Legend has it that Margarita was far more beautiful than the other shady ladies from good old Mexico. She was tall and slender with an exotic, almost aristocratic look. Her long black hair complemented her huge almond-shaped eyes. If I'm not mistaken there is a picture of her just before you turn into the gift shop of the theater. If that old sepia photo is authentic, she was quite a looker. However, what added to her success as a calico queen was her cheerful temperament in addition to her beauty. I reckon she was a firecracker."

Billy laughed at that expression. "If she was that special, I assume it didn't take her long to find work at the Bird Cage, right?"

Magnus nodded. "Damn sure did, and that is how the trouble started. According to the story, Margarita hit on Milgreen right from the first day. She had a serious crush on him, and when Gold Dollar found out about it, she warned the Mexican girl to stay away from her man. The blonde German made her point clear more than once, they say. Margarita was most likely not the kind of woman who took orders from anybody, and sure as hell not from another soiled dove. I think that she wasn't made for obeying. Gold Dollar was European and therefore as much a foreigner to this country as Margarita was. I bet the Mexican girl showed her a you-can't-tell-me-what-to-do attitude."

Billy reflected on what Magnus told him about the events that took place over a hundred forty years ago. The more he heard, the more he worried about the outcome of the story. He had a gut feeling that he wouldn't like the end, especially after reading what was written on Margarita's grave. When he studied his hands holding the coffee mug, he saw goosebumps on his arms.

"What happened between them?" he asked, his voice barely more than a whisper.

"The story goes that Gold Dollar's jealousy got worse. Milgreen must have tried to convince her that he wanted nothing to do with Margarita, but honestly, I doubt that. He was a gambler and sat most nights of the week right in the very building where Margarita seduced her customers. One evening, Gold Dollar heard men making fun of how Margarita tried to lure her lover into her bed while his common law wife worked at the Crystal Palace. Hearing this, she must have run across the street right into the Bird Cage Theatre, not trusting Billy Milgreen's oath of faithful love. She caught Margarita sitting on Milgreen's lap while Billy played poker.

Billy interrupted. "She caught them red-handed, huh?"

Magnus tilted his head. "I guess he rather enjoyed the slender girl sitting on his lap. Gertie must have been furious at that sight. Now, let's not forget that this story was passed down from generation to generation and has probably been exaggerated or the truth watered down. I tried to find out if it's true or if it's just a tall campfire tale. I haven't found any proof that this story was completely made-up, but neither have I found a newspaper article about the events of that day in the Bird Cage Theatre. But then we are talking about two whores from different countries, and maybe their confrontation wasn't worthy for the *Tombstone Epitaph* to mention in an extra article. One can only guess."

Billy studied his friend's face and he knew that Magnus was telling the truth. He had no explanation how he knew that both women had actually existed and had gotten into a deadly fight over that man. He simply knew it, and he felt as if somebody had kicked him hard. His stomach felt queasy, and it wasn't because of the food he had eaten at the Longhorn restaurant. He feared what Magnus was about to say next but he gestured for him to continue the story, nevertheless.

Billy got up and pulled a flask of whiskey out of his saddlebag. He poured two shots, knowing that he would probably need one.

Magnus smiled. "Thank you, my friend. That goes mighty fine with that coffee. They say Germans brew a good coffee, and boy, are they right about that."

"You're welcome. So, what happened next? The two women got into a serious fight, didn't they?"

"Yes, they must have. Despite her short stature, Gold Dollar yanked Margarita from her lover's lap. Most versions of the fight have one scenario in common. They all describe how the feisty, blonde German grabbed her competitor by her long hair and hurled her across the poker area, sending her crashing right into the middle of the ongoing poker game. They must have fought like wildcats, but Margarita's strength was no match against the furious Gertie. That woman must have been raging with hate. Unfortunately, she carried a stiletto hidden under her dress in the garter belt, and she didn't hesitate to draw the weapon against Margarita. The Mexican girl was unarmed, and the onlookers, including Milgreen, didn't do anything to stop the raging Little Gertie."

Billy toyed with his whiskey glass. "Oh my God. She killed her right there, didn't she? She murdered her inside the Bird Cage."

"That's how the story goes. She stabbed the poor girl with the stiletto. There are different stories about the cause of death. Some say Margarita's heart failed due to shock and fear. Some claim she bled to death right on that poker table where her lover had played cards a few minutes before. Considering the vision you had of blood dripping off that table, I assume the stiletto punctured a main artery or the poor girl's lungs."

"Jesus. I can use that shot of whiskey right now," Billy said and emptied the glass in one swig. He wasn't used to drinking hard liquor, and it made him cough. "Did they at least hang Little Gertie for murdering that woman?"

Magnus shrugged his shoulders. "Honestly, I have no clue. That's why I would like to do some research at the Courthouse Museum. If she stood trial for killing Margarita it would have taken place in the courthouse. They have archives of all the court cases. However, death sentences for women were rare. My guess is that she was deported to the Yuma territorial prison for a life sentence or at least for a few years. We might find out in the documents. There is one thing that bothers me, though. I can't help but wonder what that voice you heard the other day meant about the promise. It seems that there is some sort of unfinished business between them."

Billy looked pale. "I doubt that all this has to do with me, especially considering the fact that I'm not even American. I mean it's the first time I've been here in Cochise County. Why should I have visions or hear voices? That is something that should happen to the locals living here. It should happen to folks like you."

Magnus shook his head, obviously disagreeing. "Remember what I told you about the past and some of the spirits trying to connect to people and places nowadays? Do you recall how I explained that they are living in their old life and aren't aware that the times have changed and their life as they knew it is gone? They search for those who were with them in those days, not the ones who live here nowadays. They can't relate to modern times and modern people but they seek the people they knew back then. You must have a connection to Tombstone's past. If you do, they know it and they don't give a dang where you live now or where you come from. For them, you're still the person you were in 1882.

Billy shook his head. "Are you talking about something like a previous life?"

Magnus didn't directly answer his question. "If that voice you heard is really Margarita's, she must recognize some specific person in you. None of the people I've spoken to about paranormal events in the Bird Cage ever mentioned a woman's voice saying she'd been promised something. I have never heard of anybody being called 'Corazón' by one of the spirits. I think someone from that building's past recognized your soul, and we have to find out why she mentioned a promise."

"Why do you think we need to know about it? I'll be gone in a few days and probably never have such an experience again."

Magnus nodded. "It might be true that you will be gone in a few days. But my experience is that Tombstone doesn't let go of people easily once it decides that you belong here, and I mean the old Tombstone, not that touristy knickknack town you see now. If we find out what promise this lady's voice was referring to, we might have a chance to grant her spirit peace. If you really heard the voice of Margarita, she sure deserves eternal rest."

Billy didn't say anything and confusion raged inside his mind. He was a modern guy and a successful former manager. He had never wasted any thought on ghosts or how rough and deadly the pioneer times had been for thousands of people. He didn't know what to believe or what to think. A possible truth confronted him that was far too unbelievable for him to digest.

Hesitantly, he told his friend, “I need to sleep on this and decide after a night’s rest if I want to do more research on that matter.”

“I understand your reaction,” Magnus said and patted him on the shoulder. “Believe me, it took me years to accept that there’s a different truth out there. There were days I wasn’t sure if I should walk into a loony bin for good. I can speak only for myself. I do believe in the Buddhist principle of reincarnation, and I’m mighty sure that you are the reincarnated Billy Milgreen. I’m certain that the spirit of Margarita is caught in the building where she was murdered and has probably waited over one hundred and forty years for the one person who triggered off the deadly events. Milgreen didn’t stop Gold Dollar in her rage. Maybe he couldn’t prevent the killing because he likely never thought that the woman would actually commit murder out of raging jealousy. Maybe he didn’t actually care for either one. But there’s also the possibility that he was a coward and too scared to step between the two fighting women.

As I said before, my offer stands. If you want to find out more, I’ll take you to the courthouse archives. If not, I would accept that decision as well. This has nothing to do with our friendship. However, I’m sure there’s more to this story. Well, it’s about time I got back home for some shut eye. Give me a call if you need anything.”

“Thank you, Magnus. I really appreciate your help and I’ll consider that offer for sure. I’ll let you know as soon as I decide what I’m going to do next. Goodnight my friend.”

15

ANOTHER VISIT TO THE BIRD CAGE THEATRE

The following morning Billy sat on the porch lost in thought. The coffee in his hand was lukewarm and long forgotten. He hadn't slept much and felt exhausted. *What am I going to do? Is it really possible that I lived in this town decades ago? Could it be true that I was responsible for causing so much hate that somebody would murder a woman over it in a former life? Are there such things as former lives and reincarnation?*

Billy wasn't able to escape the gloomy thoughts, so he faced them. He wanted to pay the eerie theater another visit, hoping that everything would be back to normal and no whispering voices would haunt him this time. Who knows, maybe he had just imagined the woman's voice and the blood stain.

For a moment, he considered booking one of the paranormal evening tours, but he discarded the idea again. Billy would feel awkward sitting at a table with a group of ghost-hunting tourists trying to talk to some unseen spirits or chasing pictures of orbs and shadows they claim to have seen. He hadn't been able to convince himself to believe in ghosts, despite the weird things that had happened at the Bird Cage.

Billy checked his watch. It was ten minutes to ten, and he made up his mind to visit the theater right now before too many tourists were strolling up and down Allen Street. If he wanted to get a feel for the atmosphere in the building he had to be there before bigger groups showed up inside of it, creating a commotion.

Billy walked through the door and bought a ticket. "I've been here before, ma'am, so I'll skip the introduction, if you don't mind. I'll head into the museum straightaway."

"All right, glad you enjoyed it so much that you decided to give our theater another look-see. We have quite a few regulars here," the lady said. She looked much older than the cashier from last time. Billy smiled at her and waited until she opened the entrance door to the main theater room.

He peered into the gloominess but by now he was used to it. He looked over at the stairs leading behind the stage. Billy heard a little boy talking to his dad but couldn't make out the words. He wasn't the first visitor of the day, because the family was ahead of him down in the basement already. Billy looked up at the cribs, imagining them packed with rowdy miners and women of easy morals. He walked toward the stage but this time didn't hear any piano music.

"So far so good," he muttered under his breath.

Billy stepped behind the stage, and the slight creaking coming from the ceiling high above the faded curtains reminded him of the story Magnus had told him of the dancer whose neck was broken. Billy stepped around the backstage area and looked up. He wondered if the management had removed all the heavy sandbags once used to lower the curtains during yesteryears' performances. He sure hoped so.

He was aware that this visit to the Bird Cage was quite different from his first one. After hearing all the things Magnus had told him, it was no longer a jaunty, casual stroll through a tourist attraction. He was more aware of the shadows, and Billy didn't just look at the artifacts this time but also imagined the people as they used them. It seemed to Billy that each item spoke to him, telling the story of its owner.

After descending half the steps to the basement, the unexpected smell of rose perfume tickled his nostrils. A soft giggle arose from a corner in front of him but faded as quickly as it manifested. With one hand on the banister, Billy walked along the gambling area. He was reluctant to look at the poker table but at last he turned and stared at it. To his great relief, there was no bloodstain on the green felt table cover. He released his breath, unaware that he held it.

The perfume could be from one of the earlier visitors, he tried to convince himself. Hadn't he heard a family walking through the basement just minutes ago? He was sure the little boy had said something funny and his mother giggled in return. Likely the woman wore the perfume he smelled on his way to the gambling area. No, there wasn't anything weird happening, not at the spot where the highest-stake poker game took place nor at the little bar nor the Chuck-a-luck corner.

The German tourist chuckled. "Visions and spirits, oh my stars. That divorce must have damaged your brain to even consider believing stuff like that." he shook his head, feeling like a fool. He felt relieved that nothing unusual was going on in the basement. Billy was glad that he came back for a second visit to prove that his imagination had played some nasty trick on him. Smiling, he studied the contents of different antique items in the dusty vault cellar under the stage which he hadn't noticed during his first visit, he'd been so distracted by what he now considered visions.

The place was a mess and everything seemed to have been thrown in there without any system. Old whiskey barrels, glass bottles, a potbelly stove, and even a school bench were stored in that cellar. With a lighthearted new spring in his step, Billy turned, planning to leave the Bird Cage. Whistling a lively tune, he intended to call Magnus to let him know that further research in the Courthouse Museum's archives wasn't necessary. He took three steps, coming even with the poker table--and froze.

She looked at him, not saying a single word. Her dark, almond-shaped eyes stared unblinking. Her delicate eyebrows were drawn together in an accusing frown. Her lips curved in the most sensual way. Her skin had a deep richness about it--not just brown, but it gave off a golden sheen, a glow. Her wardrobe confused him, reminding him of the saloon girls he had seen over the Crystal Palace. Yet, it was different because of its old-fashioned styling. She stood quiet and still before him, leaving Billy to wonder if she was another employee of the Birdcage Museum.

He blinked a couple of times because her face seemed blurry. Then he recalled that he had been about to leave and took a hesitant step forward.

That was when he heard her voice. "You betrayed me, me Corazón. You promised me that you will seek justice on my behalf. I believed you, but you betrayed that justice. You said you will make sure she pays for it. You're a liar, Billy Milgreen. You lied straight to the face of a dying woman who loved you with all her heart. Cheater. But you came back, and I'll make sure this time you pay for what she did. It was your fault, and you let me down like the coward you are. You were never worthy of my love."

The smell of rose perfume drifted toward him along with her accusing words, spoken in what sounded like a Mexican accent. Strangely, he couldn't see her lips moving, but he heard her voice loudly and clearly in his head. Billy felt as if the floor beneath his boots was giving way, and he grabbed the banister surrounding the poker area. His stomach churned as he started to feel light-headed. His hands trembled and chills ran down his spine. Was it fear? Billy stumbled forward into the adjoining room where he knew the side exit would provide him with an escape from the ghostly image.

When he arrived outside in the warm afternoon sun, he continued to shiver and gag, as if he would throw up his breakfast any moment. He put out a shaking hand and leaned against the adobe wall of the Bird Cage Theatre, gasping for air.

A couple walked by and shot him a nervous glance. They stepped away from him, probably thinking that he was drunk. He couldn't blame them because he felt sick and afraid, and was mighty sure that he looked it, too.

He still smelled the rose perfume and couldn't rid himself of the woman's voice in his head. He didn't dare to speak out loud what he was thinking, but--sure enough--that beautiful woman looked familiar.

Could it be, he wondered. *Is it possible that I saw the late Margarita or am I losing my freaking mind*?

Billy walked down the sidewalk on wobbly legs. He barely paid attention to the cars driving by and kept walking and walking, barely certain of where he was headed. After twenty minutes, he arrived at the house where Magnus lived. Chaco barked a couple of times, but then the dog recognized Billy and wagged his tail.

He pounded on the screen door. "Magnus, are you at home? I have to speak to you. This is Billy."

At first, there was no answer, and Billy felt desperate. After a few minutes, Magnus appeared at the screen door wearing his sweatpants and an old t-shirt. He looked sleepy and his long blond hair was uncombed.

"Jesus, Billy, what brings you here this early?"

"I'm sorry Magnus. I didn't mean to disturb you, but I need to talk right now. There's nobody else I could turn to."

Magnus squinted against the glaring sunshine. One glance into his friend's face made it clear that something devastating must have happened to him. "Come on inside. I'll make us strong cowboy coffee. You sure look as if you could use some, and me too for that matter. It was a short night."

Billy followed his friend onto the screened-in porch and sat nervously. A couple of minutes later, Magnus put a cup of steaming coffee in front of his visitor before filling one for himself.

Billy took a sip and nodded. "Boy, this brew is strong enough to float the colt in it. You don't happen to have a sip of whiskey here, do you?"

Magnus raised his eyebrows. "Mighty early for a shot, but sure, I got one if you need one."

Billy looked embarrassed. "I know it's early for hard liquor but believe me, I really need a stiff drink now."

"What in the world is wrong? You're paler than a whitewashed adobe wall."

Billy ran his fingers through his curly hair. "I went back to the Bird Cage Theatre. Reckon I wanted to prove to myself that I just imagined all that crap about bloodstains and voices."

His host whistled and rose. "I'll get that whiskey."

When he returned, he topped off their coffee with the brown liquid. "So, did you just imagine it?" Magnus asked and took a sip of his spiked coffee as he studied his friend's face across the rim of the cup.

"You know I was mighty relieved when I didn't see anything strange at first. I was about to cheerfully walk out of the dang place when I saw her. She almost gave me a heart attack."

Magnus frowned. "Saw who?"

Billy shrugged his shoulders helplessly. "I think it was Margarita. She stood in the corner close to the poker table. Her clothes were old-fashioned, and her outline was kind of blurry, yet she was beautiful. You can't imagine how gorgeous she looked ... but she gave me the chills."

Magnus looked serious. "What makes you think it was Margarita?"

Billy laughed but it was a bitter sound. "She spoke to me, accusing me. She claimed that I betrayed her. She told me I broke my promise and let *her* get away with the killing. She didn't mention whom she meant by *her*. Magnus, she said that I lied to the face of a dying woman. She said that I betrayed justice. Tell me, am I losing my mind?"

Magnus didn't say anything for a few moments and seemed lost in thought. Did she talk to you using a name?"

Billy's head jerked up and he almost spilled his whiskey. His hand trembled. "She said 'you're a liar, Billy Milgreen.' My God, this spirit or whatever it is really thinks that I'm that gambler who was here more than a hundred-forty years ago. What am I supposed to do? I didn't do anything wrong to her. I think it's best if I leave town right away before I completely lose it."

Magnus shook his head. "I understand your panic but running away is no solution. I heard that people can be continually bothered by spirits despite leaving the place where they first encounter them. Remember, spirits aren't bound to stay in one place. They either attach to a certain building or to a certain person."

"So, what am I supposed to do? Sit here until I end up in the looney bin?"

Magnus scratched his chin. He got up, refilled their mugs, and poured each another shot of corn juice. "I still think we should do research at the courthouse. According to this story, Little Gertie murdered Margarita. I keep wondering why Margarita thinks that Billy betrayed her trust. We have to find out what promise she's talking about. Chances are if we solve that riddle and maybe achieve justice for her, she might be at peace and leave you alone."

Billy hung his head. "How in the world can we find justice for a person stabbed to death one hundred and forty-one years ago? That's worse than a cold case."

Magnus smiled. "For them, over a century of time or even more means nothing. They live in eternity. Decades are like seconds for them. As for justice, better late than never. I wonder what happened to Gold Dollar after she murdered the poor girl. I think we have to find out what kind of promise Billy Milgreen could have made to the dying Margarita. I'm quite certain that it has to do with Gold Dollar, and if we know what the promise was, we might find a way out of this mess for you."

"Jesus Christ, all I wanted was a great vacation. You know, get away from home and forget the entire mess. Now it seems I walked from one disaster into the next. I don't know why my life has turned so crappy lately."

Magnus patted him on the shoulder. "Let me call my friend Linda. She has access to the Courthouse Museum's archives. I hope we can find some answers by reading the transcript of Gold Dollar's trial. Maybe a clue about that promise pops up in them old documents."

Billy nodded and played with Chaco while Magnus called his friend.

Magnus walked into the sunny yard. "All set. We can have a look at the papers this afternoon. She said she has to do some inventory, so she would be around after closing for the day. Lucky us. That gives us enough time to go through the documents. Fortunately, we know the approximate year when the stabbing happened. That will save us a lot of time. Let's go up to the depot and have a pizza before we go there. We're supposed to be at the courthouse at 2:00 p.m., and it doesn't hurt to have a base of decent food on top of that whiskey. We don't want the lady to think that we aren't sober enough to treat the historical books and papers with respect."

Billy agreed to it right away. As a matter of fact, he felt a little dizzy and couldn't say whether it was from the shot in his coffee or from the eerie encounter inside the Bird Cage Theatre.

16

THE TRIAL DOCUMENTS

After their lunch, the two men walked down Fremont Street, then turned to the left. It felt good for Billy to walk outside in the fresh air on such a pleasant day. The weather was sunny but not too hot.

He watched his friend Magnus from the corner of his eye and realized that he was limping. "You should have told me that it's hard for you to walk a distance. I wasn't aware of it the other day when we were hiking out to Fort Bowie."

Magnus waved his objection off. "Don't worry about it. It's an old injury in my right knee which bothers me from time to time. I've been needing a knee replacement for ages but have neither the health insurance nor the guts to go in for that surgery. You know how that is."

Billy slowed down. They were right on time, so there was no reason to rush his friend into a faster pace, which would leave his knee hurting even more.

At the entrance to the courthouse, a blonde woman who stood at the door greeted Magnus cheerfully. Billy assumed that she was in her late fifties. Her figure was trim and her hair was coiffed in a modern Pixie cut. She wore black glasses that sat on the tip of her nose and gazed at the two men over the rim of them.

She shook hands with Billy. “Howdy, my name is Linda. You must be the German fellow who wants to do some research on Tombstone’s history. Good for you. It is always refreshing to get to know someone who takes the history in this town seriously and doesn’t believe every movie quote that is preached in the saloons and gun shows here.”

Billy laughed.

“Linda is a walking encyclopedia when it comes to law cases that took place in this building,” Magnus said.

Linda blushed and smiled warmly at Magnus. “Aw, shucks. You give me too much praise, handsome.”

They walked into the building. On the way to the court archives, Linda turned to Magnus. “What exactly are you looking for?”

“We want to find out if Gold Dollar stood trial here for stabbing Margarita at the Bird Cage, and if she was sentenced to prison or if the hangman had a say in her ending.”

“Wow, now that is the first time that someone wants to find out what happened to Little Gertie after she stabbed the poor girl in that brothel. Seems that folks are more interested in Margarita’s fate and the location of her grave. They forget that a murderer was running loose, right?”

She unlocked the gate that led into the office of the law clerk and stopped in front of the opposite wall which was filled with rows of law books and stacks of old documents. The two men waited patiently.

“What year did you say this crime happened?” Magnus shrugged his shoulders. “According to what I found out it would be 1882, maybe early 1883. I’m not sure about it.”

Linda pushed back her glasses to the top of her head and nodded. She pulled two thick, leather-bound books from one of the top shelves and blew the dust from the covers. Sneezing loudly, Magnus hurried to help her carry the heavy books to a reading table.

She opened a drawer and handed both men a pair of cotton gloves. “Sorry, we have to follow the rules. These documents are old, and some of the pages are brittle. If there is any information at all, it should be in one of these two volumes. I'll go back to my work. If you boys need anything let me know. By the way, I have water, soda, and coffee in my office. In case you get thirsty, swing by."

"Thanks for your help, Linda. I really appreciate it." She waved at them and walked briskly back to her office.

"Okay, let's get started on this," Magnus said and pulled the first volume toward them. Billy switched on the antique style lamp, and they flipped through the pages carefully to make sure they didn't damage the fragile documents. After two hours, they were about to give up, feeling utterly frustrated. None of the names "Gold Dollar" or "Little Gertie" or "Margarita" were anywhere to be seen.

Magnus was about to close the first volume when something caught Billy's eye. "There!" He pointed at the right page; his eyes wide with excitement. Witness Billy Milgreen was mentioned in the court clerk's neat handwriting.

"I'll be darned," said Magnus. "Looks like we found something."

They both pulled their chairs closer to the table. Magnus turned the page to the following case and read out loud:

March 26 in the Year of Our Lord 1882.

Tombstone, County Seat of Cochise, Arizona Territory.

Courtroom of Justice of the Peace Wells Spicer, Presiding

We witnessed the trial of the murder of one woman named Margarita whose last name remains unknown. She was known as a woman of easy virtue who plied her trade at the Bird Cage Theatre. According to Mister Hutchinson, he hired Margarita, a Mexican, as a dancer and to entertain the men in an immoral way. The murder took place February 15, 1882, when another woman known as Little Gertie, now nicknamed "Gold Dollar" stormed into her former working establishment, the Bird Cage Theatre and called out Margarita. Apparently, the latter got caught sitting on the lap of Little Gertie's common law husband, Mister William "Billy" Milgreen.

According to witnesses Little Gertie had repeatedly warned Margarita to keep her hands off her man. The bartender of the

Crystal Palace, Mister Levingston, appeared as a witness. He confirmed that some miners informed Little Gertie/Gold Dollar that the Mexican soiled dove was hitting hard on Milgreen again. Mister Levingston confirmed that Gold Dollar left the Crystal Palace Saloon and was seen stomping across the street toward the Bird Cage Theatre. She appeared furious and was muttering threats against Margarita. These threats were heard by numerous men inside the Crystal Palace.

When Gold Dollar was questioned, she denied murdering Margarita. Since none of the gamblers were willing to add their version of what happened in the gambling area of the basement, the Judge called Mr. Billy Milgreen into the witness stand.

Milgreen stated he was right in the middle of the physical fight between Margarita and Gold Dollar. According to witnesses both women likely fought over the favors of Mister Milgreen.

Judge: Mister Milgreen, you have to tell the truth here. Swear by God and the Holy Bible in front of you that you will tell the truth and nothing but the truth.

Milgreen exchanged glances with the shackled Gold Dollar.

Milgreen: I swear to tell the truth. So help me God!

Judge: Mister Milgreen you witnessed the fight between the prisoner and the woman murder victim. Is that correct?

Milgreen: Correct, your honor.

Judge: I'm not going to beat around the bush. It's a busy day. Did Gold Dollar, also known as Little Gertie, stab Margarita and leave her bleeding to death, then flee through the back entrance to the livery stable?

Milgreen: I can't confirm that Gold Dollar murdered Margarita. It is true that they got into a physical fight, but Gold Dollar didn't kill the Mexican girl. I have no idea who did. When Gold Dollar left, Margarita was still alive. I reckon one of her johns must have finished her off. I left the basement because I was embarrassed about the women fighting over me. I went upstairs and had a drink at the bar. I don't know what happened in the poker area after I left.

Judge: Are you sure about this, Mister Milgreen? We know that you're involved with the suspect over there, but you still have to tell the truth.

Milgreen: I have no reason to lie. I swore on the Bible. I'm telling the truth, as God is my witness.

Judge: In that case, you may step down now, Mr. Milgreen. The court of Cochise County finds Little Gertie, known as Gold Dollar, not guilty of murdering Margarita.

MAGNUS LOOKED AT BILLY, who was pale as a ghost.

Billy remarked. "Sweet Jesus, this is a perfect example of perjury, isn't it?"

Magnus nodded. To Billy's surprise his friend's eyes were moist with tears. "Good heavens, he let her down. What did you say the spirit told you this morning?"

Billy swallowed hard. "She said that I broke a promise. She claimed that I lied to the face of a dying woman, and that I promised her I would make Gold Dollar pay and bring justice upon her."

Magnus nodded. "It all makes sense now. My guess is that Milgreen had a fling going on with Margarita. Gold Dollar must have run out of the Bird Cage after she stabbed the statuesque Mexican. The stiletto has not been found, or it would have been mentioned in those court papers. Milgreen must have stayed back talking to the dying girl, which means she bled to death. I doubt that he went upstairs to the bar, but I'm mighty sure that he promised Margarita that he'll see to it that Gold Dollar gets arrested and sentenced to prison or the gallows."

Billy nodded. "And then he lied to the judge, saving a murderer's neck. What a coward. God, I really hope I'm not such a reincarnated villain."

Magnus looked thoughtful. "You know, it is said that Milgreen left Tombstone shortly after the incident at the Birdcage, and Gold Dollar vanished even earlier, right after the trial. I bet they got together again and started over in a different town."

Linda walked into the room. "Have you found what you're looking for, guys? I'm about to close up."

Magnus looked at his watch. "Jesus, it's past six already. Sorry to have kept you from going home."

Linda laughed. "No big deal, I had to catch up on some paperwork anyway, and nobody's waiting for me at home besides my crazy cat and a pile of laundry."

Billy helped her return the two volumes to the shelves.

Linda studied his face. "Are you all right? You look white as a sheet, young man."

Billy nodded. "It has been a long day. Guess I'm just tired."

Magnus and Billy walked over to the Four Deuces Saloon. They each ordered a beer and sat outside in the saloon's courtyard.

Billy seemed confused. "Now what, Magnus? What are we supposed to do now? Nobody can undo the injustice that happened in that courtroom over a century ago."

Magnus nodded. "Honestly, I have no clue. How could anyone renew that promise and keep it this time? This is a tricky situation, and I can imagine that Margarita is a very unforgiving spirit after all these years, considering the betrayal she faced. Can't blame the woman for it."

"Do you think she wanted Gold Dollar to be hanged for what she did?"

Magnus nodded. "It would make sense, wouldn't it? You know how the saying goes, an eye for an eye..."

Billy scratched the label from the glass of his beer bottle, but he didn't speak.

"What's going through your mind?" Magnus wanted to know.

Billy looked into his friend's face. "I feel ashamed, Magnus. I can't believe that the man lied to the judge on purpose, knowing that this crazy witch killed the poor girl over a good-for-nothing gambler. He was a coward, and I feel ashamed that my soul might be connected to his."

Magnus remained silent. There was nothing he could say or do to make his friend feel better. "You know, what really saddens me is that since we found out the truth, there isn't anything we can do to help Margarita's spirit. We can't punish Gold Dollar for the sake of justice. God only knows where she lived after her time in Tombstone and where or how she died."

"True. Magnus, I want to thank you for taking the time to go through those documents with me. If not for you and your friend Linda I wouldn't know what's going on with me. I admit I'm still having difficulty believing the entire story, I mean, Jesus, we are talking about ghosts here. When I sat on that plane, I never expected to step into a weird tale like this."

"I think you should go back to your rooms and try to unwind. Get some shut eye, Billy. It has been a crazy day for you."

Both men walked out of the saloon and toward Fremont Street. When they reached the San Jose House, Billy bid his friend goodnight.

Magnus turned and started to walk away but Billy called him back. "Magnus, what if Margarita won't leave me alone?"

His face looked serious when he answered. "I don't know, Billy."

The young German turned and unlocked the door. For the first time the thought of sleep was unnerving and he feared unsettling dreams.

17

CONSPIRACY

It was long past midnight, and the last evening tour inside the Bird Cage had ended three hours ago. Despite the fact that all the tourists left, the old theater wasn't deserted. Dozens of people filled the main room, the stage, and the basement. The air was thick with cigar smoke, which created a bluish fog obscuring the blurred figures of pioneers and shady ladies roaming the building.

A piano played a lively tune while the dancers swirled on the stage, lifting their skirts far above their knees, to everyone's delight. Cheering and hollering accompanied the clink of dozens of glasses toasting each other. Occasional gunshots erupted, causing the crowd to cheer and laugh even louder.

The corpulent figure of Mr. Hutchinson walked down the stairs to the poker area. He was overjoyed to see the place packed tonight. The owner rubbed his hands, knowing that he would earn a fortune again this month. Hutchinson was aware that they all were long gone--at least their physical bodies had departed. He couldn't care less. The owner of the establishment had always been reckless and greedy, and it hadn't changed with his own death over a century earlier.

The daytime tourists of modern-day Tombstone kept his premises alive. Those ignorant people with no clue about what the real Tombstone was like fed every spirit in his building with their energy. He chuckled when he saw the tourists playing with the idea of paranormal tours within these walls. One could only wonder what it would be like if the true inhabitants of the Bird Cage Theatre showed themselves openly to the crowd seeking paranormal encounters.

The twenty–first century folks probably had no idea how dangerous it could be to go ghost hunting. They felt safe and sound doing a little ghost watching and cheerfully photographed every orb they saw while not knowing that spirits could indeed harm a human being. If a ghost was evil enough it could do massive harm to people and easily damage objects. A ghost didn't even have to be evil to do so. If a spirit was angry enough or seeking revenge, they could do damage too. Oh yes, there were quite a few furious ones among them. Some of them had every reason to hate folks from their past as well as living people.

Margarita was one of them. Hutchinson, being the mean person that he had always been, even during his successful lifetime as a business owner, liked to tease Margarita. He was a cruel man, and she had been a fool to give her heart to that good-for-nothing coward who called himself a professional gambler. The hell he was a "professional." Milgreen had been nothing but a cheater with those cards as well as with the girls.

Hutchinson had been more than a little interested in Margarita, and the fact that he was married didn't stop him from pursuing her. A man would have been blind if he hadn't been entranced by the exotic beauty. She was definitely one of the most gorgeous women in town, but she'd turned Hutchinson down. God knows she could have had every man in this thriving mining camp. But nothing can be done when love speaks to a human heart, and Margarita had fallen head over heels for this Milgreen feller.

When Hutchinson arrived downstairs, he saw Margarita standing in the corner staring at the poker table. It was the very table on which she bled to death, and her blood could still be seen trickling off its surface. What a loss that had been. Margarita was one of his best ponies in the stable. When Hutchinson fired Little Gertie because her uncontrollable rage caused trouble with his high paying customers, he was mighty relieved to have gotten rid of her. Then the lunatic witch came back and murdered the most beautiful girl working in his place.

"Damn, crazy hag," Hutchinson whispered. Then he walked over to Margarita.

"So, little lovebird. Your lover seems to have come back to town, hasn't he? They all come back, don't they? Never mind how many decades it takes," Hutchinson added with dirty laughter.

"Yes, the cheater is back," Margarita answered in her husky voice that still held the slight Mexican accent.

Hutchinson smirked. "Shame there's nothing either of you can do about taking revenge. Little Gertie is gone, and she got away with cold-blooded murder, thanks to your lover, darling. He's not a man who keeps promises, is he? Swore by the Bible that he would tell the truth, and then he let you down the very same instant. You would have been much better off if you had accepted my offer to warm my bed from time to time, Señorita."

Margarita turned toward him, and the big blood stain on her rib cage came into his view. It was the very spot where Gold Dollar's stiletto had ripped through her clothes and flesh. Although the brutal stabbing had occurred hundred and forty-one years ago, it still bled.

"You are right, Hutchinson. Gertie is gone. Maybe she paid for what she did in some other town, maybe not. I hope one of her lovers cut her throat. However, I might still get my revenge, though, because he came back. If I can't bring justice upon Little Gertie, I might still be able to make Billy pay for the way he betrayed me. He hasn't shown any respect, not for my love or for the Holy Bible or the law in this town. He promised me that he would bring justice upon that murdering, ugly witch and I believed him. I died with that hope."

Hutchinson roared with laughter. "Well, he didn't keep his word, did he? Matter of fact, thanks to his lying under oath she got away with killing you. Since he disappeared a few days later, I reckon the two lovebirds got together again and probably had a good laugh on your account."

"Time will tell who will win in the end, Hutchinson. I have all the time of eternity. Now that he has come back to Tombstone, I might still be able to pay him back the way he deserves."

Although her beautiful face was blurry like a wavering image in the heat of a summer day, the dangerous, hateful glitter in her eyes was clearly visible. The sweet scent of her rose perfume couldn't entirely erase the iron-like smell of the blood seeping from the wound at her side.

Margarita smiled. "Billy belonged to me and it's about time I claim my man," she whispered, then she simply faded away. All the pioneers and soiled doves who had roamed through the building vanished as the first rays of sunshine crawled over the Tombstone hills. A new day had begun in the epic western town.

18

TRYING TO LEAVE

When Billy got up, he was exhausted and in a rather grouchy mood. The longer he stayed in Tombstone, the more he felt that a dark storm cloud hovered over him. He felt threatened and at the same time ridiculous for fearing something that didn't fit into his modern-day life.

Billy didn't know what to believe anymore. He was a modern man who had achieved things in Europe. Unlike others in this town, he didn't live in a fantasy world. He was an accomplished and smart man. *Heck I'm just a normal tourist and not one of those new age brothers who believes in tarot and pendulums.*

But then there were the things he experienced at the Bird Cage Theatre, as well as the court papers he saw and read with his own eyes, which proved the things he had witnessed in that museum. Could it be coincidence? Was his imagination playing nasty tricks on him? But what if there was truth behind it all? That was likely the thought that scared him the most.

Two hours later, Magnus pulled into the parking lot of the San Jose House. He caught Billy checking his rented Harley-Davidson. "Howdy my friend. Are you planning to go for a ride on this beautiful day? I was wondering if you would like to join me. I need to go to

Sierra Vista for a few errands, and I could show you the Fort Huachuca military base there. It's one of the oldest in the entire country that has been operating nonstop since the 1800s. They have a cool museum about the buffalo soldiers and much more."

Billy shrugged his shoulders. "I wouldn't mind doing so, but unfortunately I can't ride because this motorcycle has decided to give up on me."

Magnus frowned and got off his BMW. "What do you mean give up on you? Something wrong with it?"

Billy walked around the fender and shook Magnus 's hand. "I just made some fresh coffee. Want some?"

Magnus nodded. "Sure. Coffee is always a good thing."

Billy walked inside and returned with two mugs filled with the steaming beverage. He handed one to Magnus and then pointed to his motorcycle. "To be honest, I planned to ride out of town for the day. I need to get away from Tombstone for a few hours because all these events keep bugging me without letting up."

Magnus took a sip of his coffee and nodded thoughtfully. "Understandable. I keep wondering about the events myself. So, a trip to Sierra Vista might not be a bad idea then, huh?"

"Well, the problem is that I can't get the engine started. Battery seems okay, and I have enough fuel in the tank. I checked the tubes to see if one was loose, but there's no leakage or anything that could explain why the engine simply will not start. It's dead. Not making a sound."

Magnus frowned. "Sounds like the battery to me. You know what? I have a good friend. He's a Harley mechanic and lives down the road from where I stay. I saw him in his garage this morning so chances are that he's off today. Let me give him a call. He might be able to have a look-see and find out what's wrong with this baby."

Magnus called his friend on his mobile phone. It didn't take long before the guy showed up. He looked like the typical biker, tattooed from head to toe. His hair was short and his beard well-trimmed. Billy judged him to be in his early forties.

"Hey, my name is Lincoln. Heard you have a problem with this little drama queen here."

Billy laughed. "So far she has not caused me any drama but for some reason the engine won't start, and I doubt it's the battery."

Lincoln nodded and walked to his saddlebag. "I brought my charger along, so we'll see right away how low the battery is, once I hook it up to this fine thing here." He swiftly removed the seat and hooked up the battery of the rented motorcycle.

Meanwhile, Billy poured his guest a cup of coffee.

"Thanks. Highly appreciated. My first cup today," Lincoln said with a grin.

He took a long sip despite the fact that the coffee was still very hot. Then he set the cup aside on the porch, walked over to the motorcycle, and tried to start the engine. No sound, not even the typical stuttering when the battery was done. Lincoln looked at the charger and to his surprise it showed that the battery was almost completely full. "Nothing to do with the battery. That thing is as loaded as if it came right off the shelf. It is actually in better condition than my own. Let me quickly check the connections. Maybe one of the plugs is loose. Happens from time to time due to the heavy vibrations of the engine."

Billy was glad he was here, because the guy obviously knew what he was doing. After checking almost every wire and connection he could lay hands on without taking the engine apart, Lincoln stepped back from the motorcycle and scratched his head. "That looks kind of strange. I have to admit I have no clue why this engine is dead. I work in the motorcycle shop in Sierra Vista, and I can call my boss to pick it up and take it over there. I'll have to hook it up to our computer and likely tear half of the engine apart to get to the bottom of the problem. Since it's a rented bike, you don't have to worry about it because you are insured and the costs of repairs will be covered. After all, there's no damage from an accident or anything that could indicate you mistreated the company's property."

"You know what, Billy, since we can't ride to Sierra Vista together unless you sit in my side car, I can postpone the errands until tomorrow and give you that promised tour of the Good Enough Mine here in town. If I do the extensive tour, it will take around two or three hours. What do you say?"

Billy shrugged his shoulders. "Looks like I can't escape this town today, anyway. So yes, let's get this baby to the mechanics and then explore the underground tunnels. I really appreciate your help, Lincoln."

"It's no big deal. You know there's some truth in the saying 'Always take your tools when you ride a Harley,' " he added with hearty laughter. He dialed a number on his phone, spoke quickly to his boss, and they arranged transport for the flatbed to pick it up within the next hour.

While they waited for the truck, the three men sat on the porch and enjoyed more coffee. "Hey Linc, how does your girlfriend like her new job at the Bird Cage?" Magnus asked.

"She enjoyed it the first few days, but she got into a fight with the boss-man yesterday."

Magnus raised his eyebrows. "Why is that?"

Lincoln looked serious. "One of the artifacts was stolen yesterday, and it likely happened during her shift although there's no proof of it. But you know how it is, the new one gets the blame, although they can't say when the damn thing disappeared. Could have happened days before she even started working there. Hunley keeps so much junk in that museum that I'm astonished they even realized something was missing. I bet he doesn't know all the items in that old shack."

Billy remained silent. If there was one thing he didn't want to get involved in today, it was a conversation about the Bird Cage Theatre.

"What's missing?" Magnus wanted to know. "I know from my own job as tour guide in the mines how reckless some tourists can be. They often try to get souvenirs or leave their names written all over the place without any respect for the history those places try to preserve."

Lincoln pulled out a pack of cigarettes and offered one to the two men, but only Magnus accepted since Billy didn't smoke. "You know up there in one of the glass cabinets in the main theater room, they have some of the equipment that doctor Goodfellow used when doing surgeries in this town."

"Yes, I remember," said Magnus.

"Well, it happens that they keep a stiletto in the same display. According to Hunley, it looks more like a big file with a wooden handle and a sharp point. His family claims it's the weapon one of the prostitutes used to kill another one for messing around with her man. You know how jealous women are, right?," he added with a chuckle.

Billy's stomach dropped, and he spilled some coffee.

Magnus glanced over at his German friend. "Are you talking about the stiletto that was supposed to be used to stab Margarita?" Magnus wanted to know.

"That's what Hunley claims, and that's the very thing that is gone from the glass cabinet. The weird part is that this dang thing is locked in that cabinet, and only the owners have keys to every display and lock in that museum. Therefore, they doubt that a tourist stole that old rusty thing, and concluded right away that it must have been one of their employees. Of course, suspicion falls on the new kid in town. Now what in the world would my girl do with that old piece of junk? She's rather into jewelry or brand-new shoes and works at the museum only for the sake of the tips and making enough money to buy the tons of cosmetics she thinks she needs. I sure hope she doesn't get fired over it because it would be a pain in the derriere to face her grouchy mood for days to come if that happens. Besides, we can use the money. I'm planning to re-do our bathroom and get a nice barbecue grill for our porch."

Neither Magnus nor Billy answered, but before Lincoln could ask about their sudden silence, his coworker pulled into the parking lot ready to transport the motorcycle to their shop. The two men loaded the Harley and secured it to make sure it wouldn't fall over on the short drive to Sierra Vista. Magnus and Billy shook hands with Lincoln and thanked him once again for showing up so promptly and taking care of the vehicle. Then they watched the two men drive away in different directions.

Billy remained silent. Magnus turned to study his friend's face. "I'm a little worried about you. What do you think of that theft that happened at the Bird Cage?"

Billy shook his head. "I don't know if it's a regular thing that artifacts disappear there. I have seen a few cameras, but it doesn't really look like a quality security system. One thing is sure, it's a strange coincidence that out of all the artifacts displayed there, that specific one disappeared. Sweet Jesus, I don't know what to think anymore. You said you were worried. I'm really starting to feel uncomfortable here, or should I rather say, I feel threatened being here?"

Magnus slapped his friend on the shoulder. "You know what, let's lock up here and go over to the mine. I think we both could use some distraction from that dang brothel and its shady history."

Billy agreed, locked the door to his rooms, and joined his friend on the walk over to the entrance of the Good Enough Silver Mine on Toughnut Street.

19

UNDERGROUND WITH THE MINERS

The team working for the owner of the mine greeted Magnus warmly. Billy insisted on paying for a regular ticket and tried on the yellow hard hat which Magnus handed him. As he walked toward the entrance of the mine, Billy marveled at the hills covered with mesquite, prickly pear cactus, and blooming ocotillos. The blue of the sky was interrupted with a few puffy clouds and the majestic Huachuca Mountains stood out in the background at the Eastern horizon. A soft breeze tousled Billy's curls like a soft whisper of Tombstone's past.

Billy expected the mine to be a smaller collection of narrow tunnels probably requiring lots of bending over to walk through them. He knew the mining business had been big in those days, but he wasn't prepared for what he would see on this tour.

Magnus trod ahead into a cave-like entrance. A staircase built from metal and sturdy wooden planks led underground. The stairs were long and steep. When they reached the first level of the tunnels, Billy turned and glanced back to the entrance. He was surprised to see how far underground they already were. The cave entrance appeared far above as a circle of light no larger than his head. The tunnel ceiling was far over his head, so there was no stooping in this part of the mine.

"How deep did you say they dug?" he asked Magnus.

"Around four hundred feet, but some shafts are all the way down to six hundred feet below the surface. In some of the mines, we found an unbelievable six levels of tunnels, one on top of the other. The three biggest mines are interconnected with their systems of shafts."

"Isn't it dangerous to bring tourists in here? I mean, what if a tunnel caves in while you have folks exploring down here?"

"The tour guides check every tunnel open for tours before we allow the first people of the day to enter through that gate up there. Security is our first priority. The tree trunks and wooden beams they used to stabilize the shafts were brought here from north Arizona. It's mainly ponderosa pine, which is full of sap. Due to the dry climate down here, those trees dried so much it's as if they've petrified. They won't shrink any further. They also give us a good warning if a tunnel isn't stable any longer because the wood moves if any rocks start to crack. Look over there. See the wooden board between the tree trunk and the rock ceiling?"

Magnus pointed toward a corner to his left and Billy nodded. "These are our handmade seismographs. We check them every morning and evening. If those boards changed positions, we know that that particular section has moved in a way it wasn't supposed to. We take the safety of our visitors and our own safety very seriously. What really helps is the fact that temperatures are stable down here year-round, and the humidity is so low that hardly anything rots. If an animal dies here in those shafts, it mummifies but it doesn't decay."

"Miners, too, I guess," Billy mumbled.

"You're right about that except in those sections where the groundwater hit the tunnels. If a miner drowned there, he decayed if his fellow miners were unable to bring the body back to the surface. The fact is that more than one of those boys lost his life down here. Needless to say, the mines of Tombstone are another spooky place."

"Oh, no. You should have warned me ahead of time. At least, I would have brought the bottle of whiskey in case I get shocked over more ghost experiences," Billy answered with nervous laughter.

As they proceeded along the tunnels, they crossed a few spots where the tall Billy and Magnus had to bend down to make sure they didn't hit their heads on the rocks above them. Billy recalled that folks in the old days were shorter, so the miners were probably able to walk upright through those tunnels. When they rounded another bend, they stood in a huge cave-like room as big as a cathedral.

Billy stared at the high ceiling in awe. "Oh, my God, look at this. I never expected rooms this big down here. How many men worked on a shift? There must have been a lot of them to chisel out such a huge space."

Magnus nodded and, as usual, even he was impressed. "This mine never ceases to fascinate me. It's estimated that up to fifty men worked on one shift in the Good Enough Mine every day. Imagine, they chiseled all that out of the rock by hand. They had to get rid of all the bigger stones and rubble. Can you imagine how hard they worked, how much dust they breathed into their poor lungs every day?"

"No wonder they all got sick and died at a young age," Billy mumbled. "It must have been pretty scary working down here with only candlelight, not knowing when a shaft might cave in. I mean, chances to get buried alive here were probably not that low, right?"

"Amen to that, brother, plus, they often had terrible accidents when a team chiseled with a much bigger chisel and a sledgehammer. One man held the iron tool against the rock, balancing it on his shoulder and turning it, and the other miner hit it from behind using a forty-pound sledgehammer in semidarkness. One moment lost concentration, and he bashed in the skull of his coworker. To make things harder, they had to process the silver using chemicals. The men working on the surface weren't better off because they used mercury. At that time, nobody knew how toxic mercury is and how it causes brain damage. With prolonged exposure to mercury, they'd lose the ability to think. That poison turned their brains into a Swiss cheese."

"You know Magnus, I'm starting to understand why they didn't save up their money, but spent it on drinks, women, and gambling. It would have been rather ridiculous to save it up for a better life during retirement considering the fact they likely never reached retirement age. One thing is sure, I've gained a new respect and a different image of the miners. Now I understand why you have such a high respect for them, and try to keep their history alive by telling it to people. They deserve not to be forgotten, don't they?"

Magnus looked at his friend and tears misted his eyes. "That is exactly the point, my friend. They've worked very hard and died way too young in horrific ways. It's only fair that their history and memories are kept alive."

They continued their stroll through different side tunnels. Billy could hardly believe the extent of that mine. Magnus told him it was only one of the three major mines in and around Tombstone, not taking into account the dozens of smaller ones in the surrounding hills. According to city plans and the old historical mining documents, Tombstone hosted hundreds of miles of mining shafts.

When they finally walked back up to the surface, Billy was surprised to see the sun setting behind the hills. "Do you think there's still silver in the shafts?" he asked his friend.

"Oh yes, no doubt about that. Although this was the biggest silver strike in the entire country, geologists still assume that the mother lode hasn't been found."

"Why did they stop prospecting it, then?" Billy wondered.

"They got too greedy. By digging too far below the water table, the shafts became flooded, and they had to erect huge steam pumps to clear out the groundwater from the lower levels of the mines. It was too difficult to maintain adequate working conditions. After a number of miners drowned like rats down there, they simply gave up. An earthquake triggered more water leakage and also sent the San Pedro River underground. The redirection of the river removed the water they needed for processing in the stamp mills downstream where silver was removed from ore. The redirected river also caused more flooding in the shafts. Nature stopped them full force."

"Wow. I have to thank you Magnus. I learned more about the history here than any other visitor in this town, although, so far, some experiences have been rather scary. May I treat you to dinner for the amazing tour you gave me in those tunnels?"

"Sure, let's go over to the Longhorn. I could use some food. Walking those mines makes me pretty hungry."

When Billy returned to his boarding house he felt better. He had not thought about the Bird Cage Theatre or Margarita at all and slept deeply and undisturbed that night.

20

WHEN LOVE TURNS TO HATE

The old, haunted building lay in darkness except for the emergency exit lights. Their ghostly greenish glare spread across the artifacts, while others were barely visible in shadowy corners of the different rooms. It was quiet in the building, and completely different from the usual rowdy crowd that filled the poker area in days gone past. The smaller adjoining room leading to the gift shop was frequently filled by visitors on their way out of the building. Few paid attention to the framed historical photos and prostitution licenses hanging on the walls of that small chamber.

Sadly, most tourists were too uninterested to read the labels next to those portraits. They would rather study displays of guns or gambling equipment, and most of them didn't study the portraits of shady ladies in those old, faded, sepia-colored photos. Yet, it was those pictures that put a face to certain names mentioned in books or talked about in Tombstone.

Alongside all the others, three portraits in one corner showed two women and a man with a well-trimmed mustache, his wavy hair combed to the side. The man's portrait was flanked by those of the two women, who looked very different from each other. The one to the left showed a white woman with her hair hidden under a hat adorned with feathers. Little earrings dangled from her earlobes. Her outfit was rather elegant, and her lips curled in a slight smile. She had a pleasant face except for a pointy nose, although her eyes showed a certain coldness.

The portrait to the right was that of a dark-haired woman. Her delicately arched eyebrows framed almond-shaped eyes that were so dark they appeared black. Longing and melancholy radiated from her gorgeous features. The serious look didn't distract from the fact that she was a beautiful woman. Her lips were curved in a sensual way, and high cheekbones added to her exotic looks. Her hair was braided and piled up atop her head like a crown. Indeed, she looked like a queen from a faraway kingdom. Her skin seemed darker than the other woman's. Lace adorned the collar of her modest dress.

While the lighter-skinned woman wearing the hat in the left-hand picture held her head in a coquettish way and appeared to be flirting with the camera, the other woman wore a stoic expression. She portrayed a certain confidence that lacked haughtiness.

The security camera in the corner didn't catch the movement of the black shadow toward those three portraits. Its sensors weren't responsive enough and it had been programmed only to catch images of tourists walking by.

The shadow remained standing in front of the pictures, studying the one in the middle. A whisper spoke to the framed photograph as if it were a living person. "I gave you my heart, and I trusted you. You betrayed me, and it was you who didn't try to stop that lunatic floozy from killing me. You were not man enough to protect or to love me. Time will tell if you're man enough to die. Maybe you'll be braver when that moment comes because sure as hell you were a damn coward in your lifetime. There's no peace in forgiveness. An eye for an eye, Billy Milgreen."

The shadow formed into a woman and continued to stare at the portrait. She turned her head to the left to look at the other portrait, studying the white woman's face. Her beautiful features contorted with hate.

The two photographs behind the glass abruptly changed. A tiny black spot spread from the center of the photos, obscuring both images. It looked as if the man's portrait and that of the lady on the left had been charred by a flame. It erased the faces of the people in the photographs yet didn't set off the smoke detectors. The portraits seemed to burn with fire, although there were no smoke or flames.

When the shadow turned away, it vanished as it walked toward the poker area. Only the signs were readable under the portraits.

William "Billy" Milgreen, a young gambler that Gold Dollar and Margarita fought over.

The sign on the left read:

Little Gertie, a prostitute who worked at the Bird Cage for some time. She was nicknamed Gold Dollar.

The portrait of the dark hair beauty on the right side remained unharmed. The sign underneath explained visitors that the dark-haired beauty's name said:

Margarita, a prostitute who died while she worked at the Bird Cage Theatre.

21

OBSTACLES TO LEAVE

Magnus called Billy the next morning. "Hey, my friend, I have good news for you. Lincoln called me and promised me he would deliver your motorcycle this afternoon."

"That's amazing. Did he mention what was wrong with it?"

"Not exactly. He said it was something he hadn't seen before—something weird. He'll come by around noon and explain it to you."

"Cool. I'm relieved to hear that. You know after ten days of staying here I'm kind of getting itchy to hit the road again."

Magnus remained silent for a moment. Then he asked, "Are you getting bored in Tombstone or do you rather have the urge to leave because of the eerie stuff happening?"

That's a good question, Billy thought. He said aloud, "I think it's a little bit of everything. But apart from that, I really want to see areas in north Arizona and the New Mexico border area. I want to visit Canyon de Chelly and likely ride all the way to Mesa Verde."

"Wow, I've been there and envy you for that trip. I wouldn't mind returning there anytime. Those places are pure magic, sacred, so to speak. I'll swing by when Lincoln delivers your motorcycle, and maybe we can ride to Benson together for a meal at the Horseshoe Café. You'll love the place. They serve real cowboy food there."

"Sounds great. Maybe you can fill me in on certain places I should visit on the way to Mesa Verde. I'm very interested in Anasazi history."

The morning passed quickly, and Lincoln and Magnus arrived at the same time. Lincoln unloaded the motorcycle and laughed. "You know that little baby here made me wonder."

"Why is that?" Billy wanted to know.

"Well, remember how I checked almost every possible problem when you guys called me?"

Billy nodded.

"Believe it or not, I pushed that bitchy little thing into our shop and described the problem to my boss. He put the key into the ignition, pushed the starter and the dang thing rumbled sweetly like a purring cat. I drove it around the block and there wasn't anything wrong with it. My boss did the same, and again it functioned perfectly. So, with that being the case, we decided not to charge you anything. If you give us a twenty-dollar bill for our tip jar we'll leave it at that."

"I'll be darned," Magnus said. "How is that possible? Neither one of us were able to get this motorcycle running at all."

Lincoln shrugged his shoulders. "Maybe it wanted to be touched by the boss man. These things have their own minds, I tell you."

Magnus and Billy got ready to ride to Benson after Lincoln left. It felt good to be back on the road even if it was only for the afternoon. While having an early dinner at the Horseshoe café, Magnus asked when Billy planned to leave Tombstone.

"I think I'll head out tomorrow after lunch. I'll not ride a good distance tomorrow and stay somewhere along Route 66."

Magnus looked thoughtful. "I'll miss you my friend, and so will Chaco. It's a true pleasure to have gotten to know you in person. I think we're on the same wavelength. Any chance that you will return before you fly back across the pond?"

"I don't know yet, but since I have a three month's vacation, I might as well do that. And by the way, I can only return that compliment. It's a pleasure to call you my friend. If not for you, I wouldn't have learned so many things about Tombstone, Cochise County, and the rich history here."

The two friends enjoyed their leisurely conversation. Magnus suggested certain interesting stops en route to the Navajo reservation and the Anasazi cliff dwellings Billy intended to visit. It was dark when they rode back to Tombstone. The two friends planned to have a last breakfast together the following morning. Billy wanted to pamper Magnus for all the time he had spent showing him around.

That night Billy's sleep was deep and untroubled. The following morning, the weather was gorgeous. Birds chirped and the sun shone from a blue sky interrupted by a few puffy clouds. Billy had packed up his belongings before he met Magnus at the O.K. Café. They enjoyed a cowboy skillet breakfast and lots of strong coffee.

After a heartfelt goodbye and some extra treats for Chaco, Billy was ready to pull out of Tombstone at one p.m. He was grateful for the late checkout and thanked his host Anne McKechnie for the amazing stay at the San Jose House. He closed his leather jacket and pushed the starter after turning the key in the ignition of the motorcycle. Nothing. Billy frowned, turned the key again and pushed the starter. Nothing happened.

"Come on. What's your freaking problem now? You worked mighty fine yesterday."

He tried again and again but the engine didn't produce a single sound. Not even a light went on. "I don't believe this. Is this some kind of bad joke?"

He pulled his phone from his pocket and dialed Magnus' number. "Hey Billy, have you forgotten something?"

"Magnus, I can't leave. That damn motorcycle is on strike again."

"What do you mean by 'on strike?' It worked perfectly yesterday."

"I know and don't ask me what's wrong. I don't get it. I put fuel into the tank and checked the oil. The engine didn't give me any problems yesterday, not even a stutter. And now it's completely dead, just like it was the other day. I have never experienced anything like this, and I've been riding different motorcycles for years."

"Lincoln is at work today, but let me call his shop. They need to have a look into this. We don't want you to get stranded in the middle of nowhere when you ride out to the Navajo reservation. I'd inform the bike rental company, if I were you. They might have to send a replacement. After all, you paid for it, didn't you? Don't worry, I'll come over after I call Linc's workplace."

Billy called his host and told Anne that he was forced to stay another day or two. Fortunately, she hadn't rented the room to anyone else yet. Frustrated, he carried his backpack back into the room and took off his jacket.

When Magnus came by, he also checked the motorcycle but couldn't get it to run. Confused, he scratched his chin.

Around 4:30, Lincoln came by with the transport from their motorcycle repair shop. "Hey, Hoss, what did you do now?"

"I have no clue what the problem is. Same thing as the other day, it seems. I have never seen anything like this."

Lincoln tried to get the motorcycle started, but after a few tries, a confused expression clouded his face. "I'll be darned. What in the Sam Hill is wrong with the stupid thing? I wonder if there is a loose connection causing some kind of shortage. I reckon we'll have to take the engine apart. We are pretty much booked but I'll try to squeeze you in. It will take at least two days unless we have to order parts. In that case, it will take longer. Strange. That baby has hardly any miles on her yet. I would expect that kind of trouble with a well-used Harley, but this one is mighty new."

He repeatedly shook his head as he loaded the motorcycle. It seemed that even the mechanic was confused about the weird technical failure.

Magnus didn't feel like bothering Billy because he knew that his German friend was incredibly frustrated over not being able to get on the road as he had planned. So, he offered to help him if he needed anything. Billy knew that all he could do right now was wait until his Harley was repaired. If Lincoln's shop couldn't manage it, he'd call the rental company and ask for a replacement bike right away. He didn't want to spend his well-deserved vacation in fear of having technical problems on the road all day. It sure had been expensive enough to rent the vehicle for the three months duration of his holidays. The least one could expect was that it functioned without any breakdowns.

He called Easy Rider Rentals to inform them about the situation. They asked him to wait and see what the shop had to say about it. They promised that they would send an upgraded model for the inconvenience in two days if the Harley shop in Sierra Vista didn't return the bike by tomorrow evening. *Might as well make the best out of the situation,* Billy thought.

Around six in the evening, the still-aggravated Billy decided to take a walk round the back roads of the town. He was hoping to be able to let off some steam. In any case there wasn't anything he could do about the mess right now.

He walked along Toughnut Street toward the hills on the west side of town. The sun was setting in magnificent colors and Billy couldn't recall ever seeing such gorgeous sunsets as there were here in Arizona. He sat on a rock and marveled at the changing colors. The sky looked as if it were on fire, and Billy admired God's creation. Despite the annoyance of the day, he felt at peace.

A cardinal flew from one branch of the mesquite tree near to him to the next tree. They were beautiful birds with their fiery red feathers. Billy watched the bird and frowned. *Weren't the cardinals messengers from deceased human beings?* Billy recalled having read something about it in an article in *Arizona Highways Magazine.* Just as the owl was considered to be an omen for an approaching death within a family in many American native tribes, the cardinal was said to be a messenger of a departed person who wants to greet someone they loved in life.

Billy got up and walked through the semidarkness as the last hint of red and purple shined just above the rim of the Huachuca Mountains. He continued walking without paying attention to where he was going as so many thoughts about his past and his possible future crossed his mind. His stay in Tombstone had changed his entire outlook on this world. As much as he enjoyed staying here, it confused him.

Billy didn't know how long he had been walking through the back streets of the mining community, but it grew dark quickly after sunset. When he turned around, at first, he didn't recognize the street he was standing in. He hadn't been aware that he had strolled all the way to the end of Allen Street. Buildings were thinly spaced here, and the neighborhood looked dicey.

He spun in his tracks to take the same route back. Due to the darkness and dim streetlights, he had to walk carefully to make sure he didn't stumble in one of the countless potholes in the asphalt. After walking for some time, he recognized the buildings on Allen Street ahead of him. The Tombstone Hotel was on the right but the hotel's windows weren't lit. It didn't look as if many guests stayed there this week. Nor were there people on the street.

The Bird Cage Theatre stood to the left. A dim yellow street lamp illuminated the boardwalk a little. A bolt of lightning split the sky toward the Huachuca Mountains.

"Looks like we're getting a thunderstorm," he mumbled. It surprised him since he had not seen a storm moving in when he started his walk. No wonder nobody was roaming through town. Besides, it was one of the quiet weekdays, and the saloons didn't seem to be busy either.

Billy sniffed the air like a puppy and inhaled the smell of rain drifting toward him with the breeze. It was the odor of wet desert soil, mesquite trees, and creosote bushes. Despite the dust in the air, Billy had gotten used to the scent of the Sonoran Desert. The smell of the desert had crawled inside his head and the feel of it had settled on his skin. Germany and all the things which had been part of his life for so long felt more distant than ever.

He stood on the street corner and watched the storm clouds rolling in. A rising moon illuminated their movement across the night sky. The same moon that had shown its silvery face over this pioneer town in 1882 now lit it in the twenty-first century. *Did the people from that time stop walking at night to watch a storm brewing just like I'm doing now?*

To Billy's surprise, the sudden scent of rose perfume tickled his nostrils. He'd walked closer to the Bird Cage Theatre, where he had last smelled that fragrance.

Billy saw someone standing a little apart from the yellow circle of the streetlight. He squinted his eyes until he made out the slim figure of a woman. Perhaps she awaited someone. Her long, feminine skirt and her long, wavy hair remained still despite the stiff breeze blowing in with the storm. Her dark hair cascaded down over her back. As he approached to greet her, she spun around. To his horror, he gazed into the beautiful face of Margarita.

"Jesus, have mercy," he whispered. "I'm losing my freaking mind."

She stared at him without speaking. Alarmed, he crossed the road hoping that he could avoid the apparition, or whatever it was. *Man, it is time for you to leave this town,* he thought. *This ain't fun anymore.*

The ghostly shape flitted beside him. "Oh, Billy. Do you really think you can avoid me? Are you foolish enough to believe that it's so easy to leave this time? If Tombstone doesn't want you to bid farewell, then you won't. Otherwise, you would have left today, wouldn't you? Why do you think that wasn't possible?"

Her lips smiled, but her eyes stared at him coldly. He saw a dangerous glitter in them, but he wasn't sure. It might just be the moonlight reflecting in the translucent pupils. What did she mean that he couldn't leave Tombstone? His motorcycle crossed his mind. No visible breakdown, yet it still wouldn't function when he considered leaving town for good. Was it a coincidence? *It surely was*, he thought. However, a spark of doubt remained, since neither Lincoln nor Magnus had any explanation for the engine failure.

Fear spread down his spine, leaving a nervous tingle. Billy wished he'd wake up in his bed and discover the image of this woman standing in front of him was only an unpleasant nightmare.

"Billy, my oh-so-cunning lover, after the day you betrayed me in that courtroom, you left and didn't waste another thought on me, did you? They dug a hole in that cemetery over yonder and buried me like a stray dog. Nobody attended the funeral. Nobody grieved for me, Billy Milgreen. You and that witch both left this town as if nothing happened. You killed me as much as she did because you had it in your hands to seek justice on my behalf. You owed it to me. You promised it to me and yet you lied for her, making sure Gertie escaped the hangman. Was my life not worthy like everybody else's? Was my love not good enough for you, Billy?"

The young German felt his stomach churn. "It wasn't me. It was a long time ago. For Christ's sake, I'm not Billy Milgreen, woman." She reached out to him, her slender finger caressing his cheek. Billy felt as if an ice cube moved over his face. Goosebumps covered his arms.

Billy didn't want her to touch him. Then he froze as he realized that she was actually able to do so. If that were possible, she could likely also harm him, just as Magnus assumed. He panicked as he looked wildly around, but nobody was nearby. No locals walked on Allen Street and no tourists hurried along the boardwalks on their way to one of the saloons.

The first drops of heavy rain fell and the distant rumbling of thunder came closer. The wind picked up. *It is time to leave. Move away from her. Now*!

22

JUDGMENT DAY

The cloudburst came down hard and lightning struck near the Bird Cage Theatre. A stark shadow outlined Billy against the adobe wall. Moments later, the boom of thunder rattled the dark windows which stared angrily at the man standing in front of the building.

It took less than two minutes before his clothes were soaking wet. The driver of a passing car saw a man standing in front of the old theater. At first, it looked as if he were talking to someone, but there was no one there. His expression was frightened and desperate.

When Debbie drove by in her old beat-up Dodge Ram, she wondered why the man didn't go into one of the saloons for shelter. "Most likely everybody closed early today, just like us."

Debbie was a waitress at Big Nose Kate's. During her four years working there, she had learned to keep a safe distance from the drunk men and weirdos who sometimes showed up in town. Therefore, she didn't stop to ask the stranger if he was all right. If only she had.

The last thing she saw was him staggering closer to the door of the Bird Cage Theatre. Because of the heavy rain, she could no longer see him in the rear-view mirror. Debbie set the indicator and turned onto Fremont Street, relieved to get home earlier than usual.

Billy followed Margarita's shadow, although he wasn't astonished that the doors to the old building swung open as soon as he stepped forward. Why he followed her, he didn't know. It was as if she controlled his movements. A feeling of resignation came over him, and with it the knowledge that he couldn't escape her. Once he entered the saloon section, the door closed.

The noise welcoming him was overwhelming. Cigar smoke hung in the air, obscuring the people with its blue haze. It made him cough. Billy knew the place was closed for the day. How could it be so crowded, then? He reluctantly looked around. Dozens of men stood in the room or bellied up against the bar, toasting to each other with glasses of whiskey and rum. The *clink, clink* of glasses touching each other rang unnaturally loudly in Billy's ears. The smell of unwashed bodies, sweat, and dirt mingled with the odor of alcohol and scents of many perfumes. Some men gave off the stench of rotten eggs from their bodies and tortured Billy's already queasy stomach.

The guests spoke loudly, trying to make themselves heard over the background noise and the lively polka played by the piano in front of the stage. The stage--he could see it now. The plywood wall was gone. Six girls swirled around on stage, throwing their shapely legs high in the air doing the typical cancan choreography.

The cancan. Billy recognized it, but how could he? Memories? "God have mercy," he whispered.

Billy knew he was about to lose his mind. He looked upward toward the cribs below the ceiling. The girls there wore low cut bodices, and their hair was adorned with colorful ostrich feathers. "The Bird Cage birds," he mumbled. Some of the curtains were closed and he could only imagine what was going on behind them. The velvet material had a rich burgundy color, and men constantly walked up and down the worn-out steps that led to those loges. Sin ruled the theater, which was far from being only variety entertainment.

Margarita walked ahead of him, motioning him to follow her toward the basement stairs. Fear seized Billy. He hesitated because he didn't want to return to the spot where she had been murdered. He didn't want to experience the moments of Billy Milgreen's betrayal. He shook his head and remained standing atop the stairs. She disappeared downstairs.

A big man with small rat-like eyes walked toward him. "Ah, Billy Milgreen. Looks like you are finally back to receive your long-deserved punishment. Nobody escapes the Bird Cage's justice, my gambling friend."

Billy turned toward the man. "Who are you," he wanted to know.

"Don't you recognize me? I'm Hutchinson, the owner of this fine establishment. You have been my guest dozens of times. Well, in the old days, anyway. I wish Margarita had accepted my more-than-generous offer. Instead, she decided to throw her lot in with you and turned me down. Could never understand what she saw in you. You are a loser, Milgreen. Always were one."

Billy listened to the man talk with his mouth hanging open. Seeing the dancers through the figure of the stranger gave him chills.

The apparition went on. "You should have taken that crazy German witch with you and left this dang town before everything got out of hand. Damn fool. Well, at least you're going to stand trial today like you should have over a century ago. You were able to fool that silly judge down at the courthouse, but you can't play the same trick here. The inhabitants of the Bird Cage know your faults, and we don't forgive easily. We don't celebrate forgiveness because we don't fear damnation. We face it every night in our own little hell here. Go down there, she's waiting for you and so are her witnesses."

Billy shook his head but before he could turn around to try to escape, hands pushed him down the stairs. He screamed as he tumbled head-over-heels, arms and legs banged and bruised.

For a moment, he lay in the corner at the bottom of the stairs, leaning against the wall feeling pain in his right shoulder and back. Blood trickled from a small wound on his right temple. He shook his head to clear his vision, but the room spun around him.

He twisted his neck to look back up the stairs. "What the heck... are you bloody crazy?" he yelled back at Hutchinson, but the man at the top of the stairs had vanished. Billy heard men roaring with laughter. He tried to get to his feet.

The shadows of three gamblers sat at the poker table pointing their fingers at him. He heard their laughter inside his throbbing head. His right arm felt numb, and Billy was sure that he'd injured his shoulder falling downstairs. Margarita stood next to them, hatred written on her face. Horrified, Billy saw a blood stain spreading on her stomach. The handle of a stiletto poked out grotesquely and moved with every step she took toward him.

"I didn't murder you, Margarita. It was Gertrude. Leave me alone. I had nothing to do with it," Billy begged. He wished he could wake up from this nightmare. *If only I had never flown to Arizona. Did I really need to see those pioneers?*

Billy felt sick to his stomach, certain he would vomit, sure he was losing his mind. Was he really talking to a long-dead woman bleeding to death in front of him? Billy shook his head again and again, in an effort to get rid of the grisly images and the increasing dizziness. But nothing seemed to work.

A man in elegant black pants, a pinstripe vest, and a long frock turned at the poker table to stare at him. He wore a tin badge on his chest and a watch fob dangled from his pocket. Previously, Billy had not been aware of him and wondered where he had come from so unexpectedly.

The man pointed at him. "William Billy Milgreen, you are accused of perjury before the Court after having been sworn in on the Holy Bible. Lying under oath is a crime, mister. You have broken the promise you gave to a dying woman--someone we are all mighty fond of. Not only did you make it possible for the murderer to escape justice, but you are also responsible for the killing by keeping Margarita on a string while you cheated on your common law wife Little Gertie. You proved to be very irresponsible with respect to your associates and the law in this town. You are a sinner and a liar, a cheater and a card sharp. Since we can't sentence Little Gertie to death you are the one who has to pay her dues. God knows the number of sins you have committed are more than enough to see you hanged."

The color drained from Billy's cheeks. Waves of nausea seized him. *How long until sunrise? How can I escape this building?* All he wanted to do was run, yet his feet refused to move. It seemed as if he was no longer in control of his body. Billy couldn't recall ever having felt this helpless.

Multiple shadows moved toward him. He swiveled his head to stare back at the stairs. *I have to get upstairs and make it to the front door,* he thought. But miners stood at the top of the stairs, blocking his way. More and more shadows closed around him, chanting "Justice, justice," like a mantra of horror.

"Dear God, let me wake up. This is only a bad dream. I know it." His head throbbed painfully, and he touched his right temple. His fingers came away covered with sticky blood. His blood. Billy had never been so scared in his life.

Margarita stood apart from the men surrounding him. "See you on the other side, my Billy Boy," she whispered. Billy screamed...

23

A TERRIBLE DISCOVERY

The next morning promised to be a beautiful day. Magnus drove to the San Jose House. He planned to check on Billy and give him some news. Lincoln called him half an hour ago.

The man had been cursing like a Canadian woodchopper on the phone. "Butter my butt and call me a biscuit if I have ever seen such a weird motorcycle. If I hadn't witnessed it myself, I wouldn't believe it."

"What happened?" Magnus wanted to know. "Did you find what's wrong with the engine? I think the guy has to let the rental company know today if he needs another Harley. I sure don't get it because it functioned perfectly the day before yesterday. We rode to Benson together and there was no problem at all."

"That's what I'm saying. My boss asked if I'm back into drinking because as soon as I pushed that dang thing into our shop, he touched the starter, and the engine purred as smoothly as if nothing happened. So, now the big boss thinks I was drunk when I checked this baby over there at the San Jose House."

"That's really weird," Magnus said. He frowned and stared at his coffeemaker. "I'll pick up Billy and bring him over to Sierra Vista so he can explain the situation to your boss. We sure don't want to get you into trouble."

"I would really appreciate that. I do need this job, Magnus. I plan to get married next spring and I don't want to mess things up this time. God knows it was hard enough for me to get away from the booze, and I won't touch another drop for the rest of my life, if God grants. It would be awful if my boss thought I betrayed his trust, after he gave me another chance."

Magnus promised Lincoln he would come in with Billy before they closed for lunch. He rode to the boarding house but Billy wasn't there. "Probably having breakfast in town," he mumbled.

Since there were so few choices where one could eat a decent breakfast, Magnus looked for his friend. He started at the O.K. Café but Billy wasn't there. Magnus strolled along Allen Street and cut over to the Longhorn Restaurant. The place was busy and the flavor of hash browns and crispy bacon hung in the air. Magnus rubbed his growling stomach. He looked at every table, but Billy wasn't there either. Frowning, he stepped out onto the boardwalk.

The sudden blaring siren of the sheriff's car followed by an ambulance made him jump. Magnus hated noise, especially in the morning.

"What's the commotion about?" he wondered. The two vehicles came to a screeching halt right in front of the Bird Cage Theatre. Magnus stared at the employee who came running out of the building. Tear streaks smeared her makeup, and she was pale as a whitewashed wall. Her eyes were huge with terror as she tugged at the sheriff's sleeve.

A few onlookers gathered on the other side of the street. The sheriff disappeared inside the building. Less than ten minutes later, he came running and motioned the paramedics to quickly bring a gurney. This didn't look good, and Magnus grew nervous. None of the local attractions could stand a medical emergency with a tourist. It damaged business for days if not longer, especially when safety issues were involved. There had been a killing right in front of the old theater some years back. Although it had been over some jealousy drama among two locals, it sure left an impact on ticket sales for a few weeks. It also puts extra stress on the employee's shoulders.

Magnus knew that from his own experience as a tour guide. He walked toward Rachel who was on duty today. She looked terribly upset, and Magnus sensed that she was coping with a severe shock. When she saw him, she came running toward him and threw herself into his arms.

Magnus held the sobbing woman. "What in the world has happened, Rachel? What are the paramedics doing here?"

"He, ... he committed suicide." Magnus could barely understand the woman because she was crying so hard.

He dug in his pocket and handed her a handkerchief. "Here, girl. Blow your nose and then tell me again. Who committed suicide?"

She did as he told her and looked up at him, her eyes bloodshot and her lips trembling. "There is a man down there in the basement. Sweet Jesus, he hung himself."

Magnus stared at her in disbelief. "You just opened this place for the day. How could anybody be in there alone?" She wrung her hands. "I have no clue. Oh, my goodness, I'm going to get fired for this."

Magnus held Rachel, trying hard to comfort her. "Do you know who he is?"

Rachel described the man. "I could barely look at him. His face is all puffy and his tongue is sticking out. His eyes, my God, his eyes stared at me as if accusing me. He is tall with dark brown curls. I saw him inside the Bird Cage a few days ago. He had a funny accent and told me something about a bloodstain that freaked him out. I should have listened to him. Maybe he was depressed or needed medical assistance. I didn't take him seriously. You know how it is when you work here, Magnus. People mention weird stuff all the time. I just didn't pay attention to him."

Magnus froze. "A bloodstain? On the poker table?"

Rachel's head jerked up. "How do you know?"

Magnus shoved her aside. "Billy," he whispered.

He ran into the building. Voices drifted toward him but the main room was empty. He ran behind the stage and toward the stairs that led to the basement. He hurried down the steps.

The Sheriff turned and held up his hands. "Magnus, you need to leave, right now. We can't allow anybody in here. Forensics will raise hell if locals trample all over the place."

"Phil, I think this is a friend of mine. Have you identified him yet?"

The sheriff was about to have Magnus removed but then he thought better of it. They didn't have a clue who the stranger was, and it would save him time if Magnus could identify him.

"Alright, one glance and you are out of here."

Magnus nodded. "Thanks, Phil. I sure hope it's not my friend." He walked toward the poker table and the paramedics stepped aside.

The basement seemed too crowded to see anything at first. Then Magnus saw the lifeless figure of a man hanging from the pipes installed near the ceiling in more recent years above the table where the longest poker game once took place. Although his face looked puffy and his tongue protruded beyond his lips, Magnus recognized Billy right away. He stood frozen in shock, covering his face with his hands.

"Oh God, no. This isn't possible." Billy's vacant eyes stared straight at him, filled with an unknown terror.

"Is this your friend? Why in the world did he commit suicide?" the Sheriff asked. What in the Sam Hill was he doing inside the Bird Cage at night?"

Magnus took a step forward but the Sheriff held him back. "Although the cause of death is obvious, we need to follow protocol, Magnus."

The men from the sheriff's office untied the rope and gently lowered the body to the floor. They continued to take photographs of the body and the poker room.

Billy's friend frowned. "Sheriff, can you move down the collar of his denim shirt a bit for me, please?"

"What for? Looks like he used an old rope. I wonder where he got it from. Seems like a real antique and deteriorated one. I am astonished that it still held weight without tearing apart."

Magnus stared at the rope. "Wait a minute."

He ran upstairs and stopped in front of the glass case next to the Black Moriah carriage. A saddle and money bag that had belonged to the Wells Fargo delivery service were displayed in the case. Magnus remembered that an old rope had been attached to the saddle horn. Although the rope was missing from the display, the glass wasn't damaged and the cabinet was still locked.

Magnus was sure that the rope had been there. How could it be gone from the display but be wrapped around his friend´s neck? He had no doubt it was the very rope from the display. However ... if Michael wanted to commit suicide, he would have broken the lock to get the item.

Thoughtfully, Magnus descended the stairs to the poker area. He doubted his friend intended to kill himself. He pondered his friend's body. A terrible thought crossed his mind.

An officer took photos and the blinding flashes of the camera caused Magnus to blink. "Let me see his neck, Phil. Something smells fishy here." Magnus pointed to the throat.

The man of the law stepped forward and gently pulled back the collar. He gasped and called the paramedics over. "Look at this. Have you seen these bruises? Camera guys, take pictures of the neck under the collar."

Magnus stared at his friend. Billy's neck showed bruises on both sides. It looked like the perfect imprint of ten slender fingers. "Jesus, look at his neck, Phil. Are you sure he wasn´t hanged? Maybe it wasn't suicide."

Phil studied the dead man. "I´ll be darned if I know, Magnus. I have no clue what happened, but this looks somewhat strange. Why would he do it inside this dang old brothel, and most of all, how did he even get into the building in the middle of the night? There's no sign of forced entry."

Then the officer frowned. There was something in Billy's right hand. Phil tried to open it and had to use some force because the hand was already stiff. The sheriff made a face when he heard the bone of the index finger break. "I'm sorry, man, but I have to see what you are hiding from us."

The town's law man removed a piece of paper clutched between the fingers. "A suicide note?" Magnus asked.

"Looks like it, but wait, what's this?" He turned toward Magnus as he stared at the piece of paper. It was wrapped around an old stiletto that had turned brown with corrosion and something that looked like dried blood.

"Magnus turned to the sheriff. "Hey, that's the stiletto Gold Dollar used to murder Margarita in this very room a hundred forty years ago. Lincoln's girlfriend got fired because it was stolen during her shift yesterday, but here it is."

The sheriff unrolled the document. It looked rather old and neat handwriting in ink covered most of it. A red wax seal had been applied under the writing. Magnus gazed over the sheriff's shoulders and read along. He caught his breath, and tears formed in his eyes.

THE FOLLOWING Death Sentence has been passed upon William "Billy" Milgreen by a jury of his peers:

First, the crime of perjury or lying under oath; second, he aided and abetted the murder of Margarita by Little Gertie, also known as Gold Dollar; and third, he fled the scene of the crime together with the suspect without bringing justice upon Little Gertie.

Mr. William "Billy" Milgreen is sentenced to hang by the neck until he is dead for the following crimes.

Wells W. Spicer
Judge of Tombstone, Arizona Territory
The year of Our Lord 1882

"Sweet Jesus in heaven, I don't believe it. How am I going to explain this mess to the major?" Phil shook his head. "If I didn't know better, I would assume this was an execution. All right, we need forensics in here. We are talking about a possible murder now. For Christ's sake, what a mess. Magnus, go upstairs and tell Rachel to call the Hunley family. This place has to be sealed immediately until the guys from the Tucson laboratory are through with it. I have no clue what happened here, but the hell if I'll simply close this case as a regular suicide. This is fishy, and I don't like the way it looks at all." He pointed to the paper. "If this is a suicidal farewell note, it is surely the strangest one ever written."

However, it wasn't fishy to Magnus. He was heartbroken, yet the letter and the stiletto made perfect sense to him. Margarita must have claimed her lover. She had at long last been able to take revenge for the wrongdoing Milgreen and Little Gertie did to her one hundred and forty-one years ago.

"Why him?" Magnus whispered. "Why couldn't you have left him alone? He was a good man."

Magnus walked back across the main theater room trying to find Rachel. He caught the scent of rose perfume and heard a soft, throaty giggle. "You won, didn't you?" The feminine giggle drifted behind Magnus as he stepped out of the theater and into the ticketing area.

24

AND THE BIRDCAGE LIVES ON

The place was packed with miners and gunslingers. The soiled doves buzzed from one table to the next, smiling, flirting, kissing. The bartenders poured bottle after bottle and the dancers revealed their slender legs in stockings imported all the way from Paris.

The Bird Cage inhabitants had a reason to celebrate. Another one of their guests of yesteryear had been brought back to where he belonged. The poker table in the basement was surrounded by onlookers who cheered the ongoing game. The stakes were higher today than ever before and the air sizzled with excitement and anticipation.

Billy Milgreen held his cards in his right hand pressed against his chest. His left arm encircled the slender waist of Margarita. He gazed into her eyes admiringly. The men envied Milgreen for having won the heart of the exotic beauty. She, in turn, was smitten by the young gambler.

Margarita leaned over and whispered into Billy's ear. "Nobody will tear us apart, mi Corazón. That is my promise to you, and I'll never break my oath. You have always belonged to me, and now you are mine for eternity. We'll always be together."

The bodice of her dress below her heart showed no bloodstain. Her healing was complete.

The police department sent out a letter to the German embassy along with the passport of one deceased Billy Grienmuller. Since they were unable to identify fingerprints on the dead man's bruised neck and throat and found no trace of a murderer, they still assumed that the cause of death had been suicide. They closed the case six weeks after the body had been found in the basement of the Bird Cage Theatre.

After finding out that Billy´s ex-wife denied paying the transportation costs of Billy´s body back to Germany, he was finally cremated in Arizona. When no relations in Germany claimed the ashes, Magnus went through the complicated paperwork and received the urn after paying the cremation fees. He brought the ashes to Tombstone. A few weeks after his friend was found dead in the famous building, Magnus sneaked into the Boot Hill Cemetery one night. His dog Chaco accompanied his master who secretly buried the urn next to Margarita´s grave marker. Magnus was certain that the two souls were united in the Bird Cage Theatre and bringing the ashes here closed the circle of their tragic romance for good.

Magnus often thought of his friend Billy. He never entered the famous building again, but he paid a visit to Margarita's grave from time to time. He hoped that both souls found happiness in the eternal nights of the most notorious honky-tonk of the Wild West.

Late at night, visitors to Tombstone passing the Bird Cage Theatre thought they could smell a whiff of cigar smoke and the aroma of rose perfume. They'd hear a piano playing a lively tune, the clinking of glasses, and the pounding of dancers' feet on an ancient wooden stage.

They'd shake their heads and walk on past through the night, knowing it could only be their imagination.

RECOGNITIONS FROM THE AUTHOR

The Legend of Gold Dollar and Margarita

As for the story about Margarita and Gold Dollar, legend has it that this murder took place inside the Bird Cage Theatre during a poker game in its early years of operation. No proof exists for the details, nor are there any facts to refute this story. Considering both women were prostitutes of foreign heritage, their altercation may not have been noteworthy enough to make it into the *Tombstone Epitaph* newspaper.

A grave for Margarita exists at Boot Hill Cemetery in Tombstone. The marker reads "Margarita, stabbed by Gold Dollar." Three historical photos are placed inside the basement of the Bird Cage Theatre: one of Billy Milgreen, one of Margarita and the third, of course, of Little Gertie, nicknamed Gold Dollar. Whether she got the name from the new gold dollar coin minted by the US government that she charged for her favors or the long, golden tresses of her hair, no one knows.

Legend has it that Gold Dollar yanked Margarita off her lover's lap and stabbed her on the poker table using a stiletto hidden under her skirts. Gold Dollar got away with it by fleeing the town. Milgreen broke up with her soon afterwards.

There were limited choices for widow or divorced women to earn a living in the old days. Sometimes women were thrown out of their house, or their husband "lost" his wife over a game of poker. Gambling addiction and alcoholism were common things in mining camps.

Women were often forced into the world's oldest trade, but there were also "calico queens" who chose the profession because of its high-income potential. Females were vastly outnumbered on the frontier. In some locales, the ratio was fifty men to one woman.

Tombstone hosted over one hundred ten saloons and fourteen gambling halls. It is said that over twelve hundred prostitutes plied their trade in the town during the mining heyday, most likely even more. Some fallen angels were comparable to movie stars nowadays, and equally famous. The shady ladies mentioned in this book were real performers of their trade at the famous Bird Cage Theatre.

The Bird Cage Theatre

The famous entertainment building was indeed widely known throughout the West and even in some Eastern cities. When Hutchinson and his wife quit work at the cabaret on the East coast and opened the doors of the Bird Cage on December 26, 1881, it started as a twenty-four hour, seven-days a week establishment that soon turned into a legend.

Sadly, the proper town's ladies refused to set foot in the building because they thought it would attract the wrong sort. Hutchinson feared for his investment. The soiled doves didn't waste time flocking to the Bird Cage as their favorite playground soon after. They were exactly the "wrong sort" the proper ladies wanted to avoid.

Not only drinks were served in the theater, but also other pleasures were offered to the gents in thirteen small "cribs" overlooking the stage area. These tiny loges gave the theater its name. The girls adorned with colorful feathers in their hair reminded the men of little birds in birdcages up there under the ceiling high above the theater floor.

The famous song "A Bird in a Gilded Cage" is based on the Bird Cage Theatre's history. Those cribs and two larger bordello chambers in the basement speak a clear language of the building's sinful past.

The longest poker game of frontier times was held in the basement of that very building. Legend says it lasted more than eight years, five months, and three days, and was never interrupted, not even for the carpenter work necessary to finish the hardwood floor. Hence, a small section is still dirt floor.

Approximately one hundred forty bullet holes can be seen in the walls, floor, and ceiling. An estimated twenty-six people were killed in the theater during its heyday. This violent past offers an impression of how rough the mining boomtown had been.

The premises were known even in St. Louis and famous entertainers performed at the notorious theater. A local legend says that Caruso sang on the very stage in Tombstone on a stopover to California. A cancan group performed in the theater wearing original costumes imported from France.

Unlike many of the structures built during the silver boom along Allen Street, the Bird Cage Theatre with its adobe walls never burned down. Two huge fires raged through Tombstone, destroying entire blocks in the first few years of the settlement. The theater and brothel closed in 1892 when the major mining corporations gave up on their mines due to groundwater flooding and dropping silver prices on the world market. Strangely, the guests at the Bird Cage Theatre seem to have risen from their chairs and left everything behind, even half-emptied glasses and playing cards.

The history of the building itself is amazing. Nowadays the Bird Cage is one of the most amazing museums found in the Southwest. The fourth generation of the Hunley family owns it. The many items on display include weapons, clothes, household gadgets, musical instruments, gambling equipment, and more. One of those items is an antic stiletto which the Hunley family found behind the building when they cleaned up the lot one hundred and twenty years later. It is assumed that this very stiletto is the weapon Gold Dollar used and threw away while fleeing the building. It is displayed in the museum.

Visitors to the museum can experience insights into daily life and the hardships during Tombstone's rowdy past.

These days, the Bird Cage offers paranormal tours as well, and for good reason. In the mid-nineteen-fifties, locals living in Tombstone avoided walking by the boarded up old building. Despite the fact that it was closed to the public, people claimed that they heard piano music at night, the clinking of glasses toasting, and the giggling of women coming from the inside of the building. The elder citizens of Tombstone feared the old theater.

Over the course of decades, many people have witnessed paranormal activities. Modern techniques make it possible to take pictures of ghostly orbs, shadowy figures, or moving shapes, especially around the funeral hearse.

Famous ghost-hunting TV productions have shot investigative series at the theater. People witness orbs, weird lights, piano music, traces of different perfumes, women laughing, transparent shadows, and whispering voices. Visitors smell cigar smoke in a building with strict nonsmoking rules. The camera crews have often experienced trouble with their equipment. Batteries in their cameras discharge rapidly despite being fully charged and unused spare battery packs lose their power as well.

The Bird Cage remains one of the most inspiring places to explore as a Western writer. Although I've visited it countless times, I never grow tired of walking through it. It's a must-see for me during each Tombstone trip, offering a window into the pioneer past.

The Black Moriah

The most precious artifact displayed in the museum is the funeral hearse known as the "Black Moriah." It had been the last ride for most of the people passing away in town during the silver boom. Its value as an artifact, as well as appraisal for the gold and silver trim, runs around two million dollars, according to the insurance purchased by the Bird Cage owner.

The Black Moriah is the last of its kind built by James Cunningham and Sons in Rochester, New York. The undertaker Watt & Tarbell in Tombstone bought it for eight thousand dollars. Tom and Frank McLaury, both killed by the Earp brothers in the famous O.K. Corral gunfight, were transported to Boot Hill in this very hearse. A team of black horses pulled it to its destination. The rig fit through the double doors of the undertaker's on Fourth Street between Allen and Toughnut.

The Goodenough Mine

The mine has been cleared of rubble and rocks requiring many months of backbreaking work. Now visitors are able to explore some of the tunnels and chambers underground. The mine tour is an amazing adventure offering a glimpse into the history of the silver mining industry. If converted to today's currency, $657 million worth of silver and other precious metal was extracted from the Tombstone mines.

The lowest tunnels are over four hundred feet deep. Six levels of tunnels were hand chiseled out of the rocks in the surrounding hills. When the miners dug down low enough to reach the water table, the rising water became an increasing problem. Ultimately, further mining became impossible when the huge steam pumps couldn't drain the water fast enough.

In Tombstone, the average life expectancy of a miner was thirty-nine years. The soil and rocks contain silica, which causes severe lung damage when breathed in over the twelve-hour-a-day shifts. The resulting disease, silicosis, causes slow agonizing suffocation and increased susceptibility to tuberculosis, which was pandemic at the time.

In addition, processing ore used the element mercury. Skin exposure and ingestion caused deadly brain damage. Many deadly arguments were settled by gun or knife. Miners came from all over the world, mainly central Europe. Thousands worked in the town of Tombstone. They are long gone but not forgotten and their story should be told.

ACKNOWLEDGMENTS

My special thanks to my friend E.H. Alberts (Magnus Alberts in this book) who shared his knowledge about the miners as well as paranormal experiences with me. He and his dog Chaco are both very precious friends and true Tombstone icons.

Special thanks to the Hunley family who keep the history of the Bird Cage Theatre alive. Gratitude and thanks to the epic town of Tombstone, my home away from home.

ABOUT THE AUTHOR

As someone born and raised in Germany, author Manuela Schneider's love of Native American and Western history might be surprising to some. But her fascination with pioneer life, cowboy heroes, and treacherous outlaws have been her constant companion for as long as she can remember.

Schneider recalls American TV shows like *Gunsmoke, Little House on the Prairie* and *Bonanza* mesmerized her as a child.

In her adult years, Schneider fueled her deep interest in the American West by traveling to the US and visiting historic sites like Tombstone, Monument Valley, and the towering sandstone cliffs of Kanab, Utah.

Experiencing the wild beauty of the Southwest firsthand made her desire to write stories of love, struggle, and survival in the wild, wild West even stronger.

After leaving a successful career in designing motorcycle fashion for the European market, Schneider penned her first Western novel in 2017. To date, Schneider has written five books that often feature strong female characters who are immersed in a battle against hardship, riddles, and deception while searching for true love and a better life. Drawing energy from powerful pioneer women of our past, this vibrant author creates captivating sagas that ultimately leave readers wondering, *Will the story continue?*

Three new books are in the publishing process at present. Another four manuscripts are expected to be completed by summer 2024. Each published book has won awards at different festivals.

Her debut as a songwriter with "Miner's Candle" and its accompanying short film has achieved great recognition and multiple awards in Arizona, Texas, California, New Mexico, and Europe. The song is played in seven countries worldwide.

When not researching or penning riveting stories about Western boomtowns and Native American life, Schneider can be found traveling all over the world or studying at writing workshops. She also writes a Western travel blog on her website, http://www.manuelaschneider.com

Made in the USA
Middletown, DE
04 September 2024